By the same author

Vengeance in his Guns
The Courageous Breed
Taggart's Revenge
Trails of Fate
Blood Quest

The L

Jim Gannon had pai
between those who k
it. Finally freed from
try and rebuild his li
Jim and he gave in to
and, plagued by his co
bottom.

Just as he began to
towards recovery, fate
unpleasant personal tru
kind of man he had bec

Finally, he was faced
stay in order to attempt,
Apache renegades, to ato
choice, lead would fly and

The Long Ride Back

PETER TAYLOR

ROBERT HALE · LONDON

First published in Great Britain 2001

ISBN 0 7090 6975 8

Robert Hale Limited
Clerkenwell House
Clerkenwell Green
London EC1R 0HT

Typeset by
Derek Doyle & Associates, Liverpool.
Printed and bound in Great Britain by
Antony Rowe Limited, Wiltshire.

To Lynn and Mark Coleman, also Lynn's mum.
Always loyal to their friends

1

Jim Gannon raised a hand protectively to shield his eyes from the hot Arizona sun. The guard, who had opened the gate of Yuma prison for him, came out to stand beside him and chuckled to himself.

'Feel reborn, do you?' he grunted sarcastically. Feel reformed by your sojourn in our house of correction?'

'Feel cleaner,' Gannon said, meeting his scornful gaze. 'At least I get to leave this hellhole . . . unlike some, huh!'

The guard's lower lip curled resentfully. He was a big, burly fellow employed for his physical presence rather than for what was between his ears, and now he was struggling for a rejoinder. Finally, he settled for his standard platitude for departing convicts.

'You'll be back, Gannon! They all are. It's just a matter of time.'

'Not this pilgrim,' Gannon said, concentrating his gaze on the horizon again as though expecting an omen to appear in the emptiness.

'What they all say. You ain't got no money and you'll try to get some. That's how it always is with your kind.'

'Well, for sure I ain't going to rob no more banks,' Gannon said, speaking more to himself than the guard.

'Gonna get a proper job, huh!' the guard said in a scoffing tone. 'Gonna settle down like honest folk!'

'Got leanings that way.' Gannon snapped back at him. Even as he said it, he wondered why he was reacting, bothering to justify himself to this clod of a guard; he hoped it wasn't that he didn't really believe it, and was trying to reassure himself.

'Straight off, your friend's let you down,' the guard whined with an air of self-satisfaction of one who knows. 'He was supposed to meet you, wasn't he? That's how it all starts, see. Unreliable friends.'

'Think again, Socrates,' Gannon said, pointing. 'That's him coming!'

The custodian followed his pointing finger along the broad, dusty trail that stretched from the gate to the horizon. A rider was coming in trailing an empty saddle horse behind him and both men watched in silence as the distance diminished.

'Mex, ain't he?' the guard said as the rider's features became more distinct. He screwed up his face and spat. 'Can' trust them greasers an inch. Mister, you ain't got much going for you if that's the best you can do for a friend.'

Gannon eyed him up and down. 'Better him than a big bag of wind who gets his thrills locking men up.'

The guard reddened. He wanted to strike out but resisted the impulse. Instead, realizing his excuse for a break from his monotonous routine was over, he turned, ambled back inside the gate and put his key in the lock.

'Money! That's the root of it!' he shouted, unable to resist a parting shot at Gannon's back. 'And that's why you'll be back!'

Gannon just kept walking. After two years restricted by those bleak walls, he felt strangely disorientated, and was struggling to adjust his perspective now. Suddenly, there were sweeping vistas on all sides, with the unaccustomed freedom to keep on walking, as far as his eye could see if he so desired. And there was that serene absence of prison sounds. No more discordant jangling of keys, no more shouting, just the peace of God's universe enhanced a thousand times to the senses of a man who had been deprived of it. That alone was incentive enough to go straight, never mind the thinking he'd done in the last two years. He just hoped the Mexican, the only one of his erstwhile companions who'd bothered to visit him while he was in Yuma, would understand, and would perhaps even go along with him.

The Mexican reined in, dismounted and made a great show of embracing Gannon.

'Mendoza is so sorry he is late,' he said. As was his wont, he flashed the pearl white teeth which he considered part of his charming front.

'No sweat. After two years, what's ten minutes,' Gannon said with a smile. 'You're looking good, *amigo*.'

He was aware the Mexican was studying him, looking for changes, and he knew exactly what he was seeing. Some meat had fallen off what had been a powerful frame; that was due to hard labour and poor food. But he was still wiry. His hair was just as blond. His nose had a definite ridge that hadn't been there, the legacy of a prison fight. If Mendoza was perceptive enough he might read in his blue eyes that his spirit, if not broken, had bent a little and wasn't burning with the same brightness as before. That change in himself, he put down to the self-examination he'd pursued during those long hours alone in his prison cell and his arrival on the cusp of middle age without anything to show for it but a doubtful past.

He gingerly mounted the free horse and eased it alongside Mendoza's. Then, at an easy canter, they started back the way the Mexican had come. Though he had no idea where they were headed, he didn't initially care very much and just enjoyed the ride. Eventually though, after a little idle banter, he broached the subject with Mendoza.

'I take it by now you got a place to hang your hat, my friend. It will be good to put my head down in a proper bed.'

Mendoza looked at him sheepishly, witholding a smile. Gannon read the expression, which rendered the answer superfluous.

'These are hard times, *amigo.*'

Gannon sighed. 'Meaning you spent all your ill-gotten gains. What you been doing these two years for God's sake? None of this came up on your visits.'

'Like I told you, the old gang broke up,' Mendoza said with a shrug. 'Since then I do a little here, a little there. Is not like the old days, Jim.'

'You're living rough,' Gannon stated ruefully.

'Pretty much so ' Mendoza agreed. He partially showed his teeth. 'But now you're out, maybe we get lucky again yes?'

Gannon narrowed his eyes. 'I'm done with bank jobs and rustling, Mendoza. There comes a time when a man needs peace in his life. What I want is a steady job.'

'*Sí! Sí!* No more banks,' the Mexican agreed. His eyes shifted to Gannon's and quickly away again. 'There are other things we can do, huh, Jim?'

'Don't misunderstand me,' Gannon stated flatly. 'I mean it when I say I want to travel the straight and narrow from now on.'

Mendoza was quiet for a moment, then said, 'There ain't much straight work for a poor Mexican and a man just out of Yuma that pays more than chicken feed.'

Gannon reined in. The Mexican did likewise, and manoeuvred his horse alongside. Gannon was figuring he had to get what he was thinking off his mind. The Mex had his faults but he'd been loyal. Unlike the other members of the old gang, he'd visited him in jail. He'd met him today too, with a horse to boot, keeping his promise. He didn't deserve misunderstandings that might prove contentious later.

'You were lucky you weren't in on that botched bank job,' Gannon said. 'I was the only one caught and two years in Yuma ain't no picnic. No way I'm ever going back so if you and me ride together it's gotta be strictly legal. Don't doubt that, *amigo*!'

Mendoza pursed his lips, looked thoughtful for a moment. 'Maybe we can try a little straight work, see how it goes.'

It was an answer which didn't carry much conviction but Gannon decided it would do. He knew the Mexican: he was never one for responsibility, and would likely struggle to adapt to a routine existence. But he owed him something and at least he'd made his position clear so there could be no recriminations.

'Let's go then,' he said. 'There's still a few temptations I ain't put aside.'

Mendoza gave his teeth their full glory. 'Careful Jim. There'll be the devil to pay.'

'To hell with old Diablo,' Gannon came back. 'Seen enough of him in Yuma these past two years.'

Three months later, footloose in the Sierra Madre mountains, Gannon was remembering that conversation with Mendoza on the day of his release and his optimism at what he had hoped would be a new dawn for him. Had he been naïve? He and Mendoza had tried an assortment of jobs in the interim and none had lasted. Mostly it had been short-term work for low pay. On the one occasion they'd found reasonable work which could have led to permanence, the Mexican's penchant for the boss's daughter had brought about dismissal by an irate father.

From his blankets, he studied the ramshackle cabin where they'd ended up after their last job had gone west. It had only half a roof and at one end most of the wall was missing. He figured it had once been a line cabin where lone cowboys would spend solitary nights dreaming of the comforts and companionship of the home ranch. At least they'd had that incentive to tough it out here.

Mendoza was absent, gone hunting. Unlike him, the

Mex didn't seem to mind the way they were living too much. The disparity in attitudes, he put down mainly to the fact Mendoza was younger. Of course, the Mex had been humouring him that first day, hoping it would just be a matter of time before he'd relent, return to the old ways, those days when tomorrow had been but a speck on the far horizon he might never reach.

Through a gap in the wall, he saw Mendoza riding in, and watched him dismount and tie his horse. When he came through the door, he was carrying a dead rabbit which he threw on the floor.

'Rabbit stew again,' he muttered. 'I think our ears are growing bigger, huh!'

'Not like our pockets,' Gannon opined. 'They're just shrinking.' He climbed out of his blankets and piled wood for a fire.

Mendoza flashed his smile. 'I have an idea to make us some money, *amigo*.'

'Inspiration, was it?' Gannon grunted as he put a match to the gatherings. 'Or perhaps a vision out there in the hills. They say that can happen when you're starving like we are.'

Later, after they'd cooked and demolished the excuse for a rabbit, Mendoza went further.

'You know my mother was Chiricahua Apache,' he stated, 'though from my beautiful Mexican face you would not know this.'

'Sure I know,' Gannon retorted, though in fact it was news to him. 'Accounts for your bandy legs, don't it?'

Mendoza laughed at his own expense, then continued. 'Today in the hills I ran into a bunch of my mother's people. They'd busted out of the reservation.'

Gannon raised his eyebrows in surprise. He didn't like the sound of that. Things had been peaceful for a while but, with Apaches loose and not far away, you'd have to keep looking over your shoulder.

'They let you live to tell the tale?'

'One of them was a cousin. He had a proposition, a way to make us some money.'

Gannon spat out a piece of bone and stared hard at his companion. 'Doing business with those renegades is a bad idea.'

'Not for me,' Mendoza said. 'They will not harm me, nor any friend of mine.'

'Like as not they're after guns,' Gannon mused. 'Guns to kill Mexicans and gringos. That it Mendoza? Is that your business proposition?'

The Mexican spread both his hands palm upwards and hunched his shoulders in a gesture of innocence.

'Would Mendoza agree to something so treacherous? You do me a great disservice, *amigo.*'

'What then? What can we give them that they're going to pay for?'

'Whiskey! Mescal!' Mendoza replied enthusiastically. 'They will pay us gold coins for firewater. That's the deal.'

Gannon looked sceptical. 'Stolen money, huh?'

Mendoza sniffed. 'One time you weren't so fussy, Jim. All money gets stolen sometime one way or another. It is the way of the world. I think maybe you have forgotten this.'

In the ensuing silence, Gannon heard his stomach

rumbling its continuing dissatisfaction as he let his eyes drift around the remnants of the cabin. He'd graduated from his cell in Yuma to this; it seemed only a small step up in the world. Where had all his good intentions got him? Rock bottom was where. Perhaps Mendoza's idea of a trade would help them get started on an upward path, and what real harm could giving booze to Apaches do anyway? If they didn't, somebody else would.

'Where'd we get the booze?' he said eventually, his voice circumspect. 'Supposing we decided—'

Mendoza came back at him as quick as a lizard's tongue. 'I know a merchant, an old friend. He will take a cut but we'll still have enough to live high for a few months.'

Gannon poked at the remnants of the fire with a stick. The evening was drawing in and he could feel its chill already. He shivered and threw more wood on the fire. Like his thoughts, the flames danced in a desultory fashion.

'I'll think on it some more,' he muttered.

Mendoza climbed into his blankets and snuggled down. Watching him, Gannon thought he detected a ghost of a smile flit across his face, as though he already knew he would agree to it. It struck him that this moment was perhaps what the Mex had been waiting for, had known it would come sooner or later.

'Don't take too much time, Jim,' he said as he turned over. 'I got a rendezvous fixed in three days' time.'

The freight wagon rattled over the undulating trail, bottles knocking together in their cases with a discordant clinking each time it hit a new bump. The noise exacerbated Gannon's already irascible mood. Though he'd agreed to Mendoza's plan, part of him was angry with himself. He was remembering the saying, 'the road to Hell is paved with good intentions', and wondering if he was already on that road now. Stupid as he was, the sententious guard on the day of Gannon's release at the gates of that other hell, Yuma Prison, had preached the cause of his downfall would be money. He'd hate for him to be proved correct.

But it was too late now to change his mind. He'd just have to hope the business with the Chiricahua would go smoothly, and have no consequences. Afterwards, with some money to get him over this bad patch, he wouldn't give way to temptation again. What Mendoza did then, was Mendoza's business.

He was still troubling over it when the four Apaches stepped out of the cluster of rocks up ahead and stood on the trail. Only one of them was carrying a rifle which he held low at his waist. Gannon figured he was their leader because the others were standing back a pace, as though in deference, and an Apache didn't show deference easily, even to a chief.

Mendoza slowed the wagon and brought it gradually to a halt. The Apaches made no attempt to close the twenty yards between them and the wagon. They just kept watching, waiting for Gannon and Mendoza to make the first move.

'The one on the left is my cousin,' Mendoza said, putting the reins aside and climbing down. 'The one with the rifle is Chato, the chief.'

'What do I do? Gannon asked. 'Sit here, like a monkey?'

'Best you come with me,' Mendoza told him. 'They trust me but they may have a little doubt about you, *amigo.*'

'Now you tell me!' Gannon said and eased himself down.

Together they walked towards the renegades, Gannon thinking how easy it would be for them to shoot them down and just take the wagon. Slyness was one of their known characteristics, venerated as a virtue amongst their kind. Fortunately, when it came to trading they probably couldn't afford to lose credibility. Blood ties were important to them too and they were unlikely to turn against Mendoza without good cause.

The Mexican halted in front of the chief and raised a hand in greeting. Chato reciprocated with a curt nod of his large head.

'This is my friend, Jim Gannon,' Mendoza said.

Chato's gaze strayed momentarily from the Mex to the whiteman. Though it was the briefest of inspections, Gannon felt the look had penetrated to his soul, that he had been balanced, weighed and parcelled up. He sensed the chief had him down as a man who would put money above his honour and it left a bitter taste. Probably, in spite of Mendoza's Apache blood, they had both been confined to that category.

'You have brought whiskey and mescal?' Chato's manner and tone were perfunctory.

'Just as I said I would,' Mendoza told him, with a smile which to Gannon seemed a wasteful superfluity, unlikely to warm his frozen-face blood brothers.

Chato inclined his head towards his right and the Apache there strode towards the wagon. All of them watched as he lifted the cover and inspected the cargo. Opening one of the crates he removed a bottle, pulled the cork with his teeth and took a generous swig. When he'd replaced the cork and the bottle he walked back and, after a confirmatory nod in the chief's direction, resumed his position.

Chato said, 'The firewater is good.'

Then Mendoza's cousin stepped forward, pulled a poke from his shirt front and tipped gold coins on to his palm. Replacing the coins, he handed the poke to the Mexican.

'The firewater will warm you during the cold, mountain nights,' Mendoza announced with an obsequious movement of his head, as though he felt the need to say something to the stern-faced warriors in front of him.

'This is the last time we will trade for it,' Chato said sharply. 'It addles the brains of my warriors . . . makes them crazy.'

'Then why give it to them?' Gannon said, surprising himself.

Chato's eyes moved over him with an air of superiority, his expression indicating the answer was obvious to a man with brains.

'Sometimes a leader has to bend or he breaks those who are not as strong as he is. But next time, Gannon, bring Winchesters and I will pay you well.'

Gannon said nothing. He had no intention of trading guns to Chato. Mendoza, he couldn't speak for, but this would definitely be his last time. Chato, he realized, would suck them in if he could; probably this day's business had been his way of feeling them out. First booze, then weapons. Give them a taste for money and they'd be back for more. But he wasn't going to fall for it and allow the man to play him like a fish.

One of the Apaches fetched the saddled horses they'd hitched to the back of the wagon and handed them the reins. With Chato and his men looking on impassively, they mounted up.

'Remember! Winchesters next time!' the chief called out as they spun the animals away.

Until there was some distance between themselves and the renegades, they kept up a fast pace. With each mile, Gannon felt his relief growing. He'd heard of Chato; he knew he'd broken out of the resevation before, unable to accept the new ways he was expected to follow. Others of the same mind had taken to him as their natural leader and joined him. Gannon could see why, now he'd experienced for himself his charisma and sensed his native cunning.

'Nice relations you got on your mother's side,' he said jocularly to Mendoza. 'Real warmth of personality there.'

'We ain't that close,' Mendoza answered. 'A shared grandmother don't exactly make us kissing cousins.'

Gannon sighed. 'Well, at least we got what we wanted from them and no harm done I suppose.'

'Is right!' the Mex said. 'Now we can live it up a little.'

'We should save the money,' Gannon opined, 'seeing as we know how hard it is to come by.'

'Not me!' Mendoza snorted. ' You're a long time dead, Jim. Money don't do you no good in the grave.'

Gannon didn't comment. He already knew they were different people. In the past he'd been like the Mexican and couldn't blame him too much for his point of view. It would be the pot calling the kettle black.

A little later, sure of his own mind, he decided to make sure the Mex knew where he stood, and that he wasn't for turning. In a tone that left no room for doubt, he said. 'I'm saving my share of the money.'

They made camp for the night in the old cabin where Mendoza had brought the news of his first meeting with his cousin. Gannon had difficulty sleeping, and when he did drop off, he had a dream. He was back in his cell in Yuma Prison, the guard leaning over his narrow cot with a smirking told-you-so expression on his ugly face. He came out of the dream in a sweat, disturbed by a gathering wind which was moaning and wailing through the rotting walls of the cabin as though in complicity with his conscience, a physical manifestation of its displeasure.

Turning over in an effort to shut out the wind's overtures, he opened his eyes briefly and realized Mendoza wasn't there. Where his blankets had been, in the pale light of the moon, he saw a pile of gold coins. Suspicious and perplexed, he pulled his Peacemaker from its holster and rose to his feet.

A glance outside, to where they'd tethered the horses, told him Mendoza's was missing. He was certain then that the Mex had decided to go his own way, and reflected that really it had only been a matter of time anyway. He'd probably known better than Mendoza himself it would come to that. The surprise was they'd managed to stick together through their recent bad patch. Once the Mex had the taste for easy money again, something had to snap.

He stooped to pick up the coins. When he counted, just as he'd expected, it was exactly his share. The Mex had been fair, perhaps because he feared he would come after him but – as he preferred to think – more likely because they had been friends and shared good and bad times. There could be a certain honour amongst thieves, as Mendoza's actions had just proved. He wished him well, and hoped he'd come to his senses before life led him down a blind alley and left him no room to turn around.

He climbed back into his blankets with an overwhelming sense of loneliness. He had no family of his own and the Mex, however unpredictable, had been his only friend left from the old gang. He tried to sleep but the woman's face swam into the lonely emptiness of the night, as it so often did these days, to plague his imagination with the kind of life he might have had if he hadn't been so wild. With an effort of will, he banished thoughts of her, telling himself practicalities, not a conscience about leaving her nor nostalgic daydreams, should be his priorities if he was to make something of the rest of his life.

At first light he rose, made himself a cup of strong coffee, then saddled up and rode away from the cabin. Once at the top of a ridge, he reined in, glanced back at that relic of a building and promised himself one day he'd build himself something more substantial, something he could call a home of his own.

Two days elapsed and Gannon was feeling better. He'd slipped up allowing Mendoza to persuade him to trade with Chato but they'd got away with it, no harm done, and he liked the feel of those gold coins in his pocket; they could maybe buy him a decent start somewhere.

The surrounding landscape was familiar – not too far from Tucson where he'd spent his younger days and where he'd known the woman. He was thinking on that when he spotted the wisp of smoke rising like a wraith on the horizon. It gave him a bad feeling in the pit of his stomach and his initial instinct was to ride on, ignore it. Yet, in the way a man is compelled to do something, even though he knows it might be for the worst he rode his horse to high ground to have a better view.

The ranch was a mile off and it was ablaze, clouds of black smoke circling the main building as though they had a life of their own that needed a cruel satisfaction. Then he realized the place and the intervening ground had a familiar look; he remembered, long ago, he'd been acquainted with the couple who owned it. They'd been hard-working folk and he guessed they'd have a family by now, probably six kids, some of them full grown. They'd had that cosy, settled look about them, even in those early days.

He jerked on the reins, intending to ride on and mind his business, but curiosity and conscience combined to persuade him otherwise. He swung back again remembering that code which decent westerners subscribed to, which said you never left people in trouble out in the wild country because next time you might be the needy one. It was that which finally persuaded him to head for the ranch.

He took a wide, sweeping approach, progressing towards the buildings in ever decreasing circles aware the fire could well have originated from more sinister sources than natural. As he rode, his eyes ceaselessly scanned the ground, searching for signs of human intruders. Halfway in, he cut across tracks that told him five horsemen had riden in within the last few hours, and had returned the same way. When he dismounted for a closer look, two sets of prints were from unshod ponies; like a knife between his ribs, the word Apache, with all its connotations, sprang into his mind making him fear the worst.

Whoever had made the tracks were long gone so, abandoning caution, he rode on in at a gallop. He was as near as he could get to the main building which was a blazing conflagration, ecstatic flames devouring it like a ravenous animal that will not be denied its need. With the heat and billowing smoke, Gannon knew he hadn't a hope in hell of getting anywhere near enough, and knew that anyone trapped inside would be dead anyway. It seemed his diversion had been wasted; there was nothing for him to do here.

His concentration moved away from the blaze and alighted on a figure lying motionless fifty yards from the main house. When closer, he realized it was a woman sprawled face-down. Fearing the worst, he dismounted, bent close and felt for her pulse. He couldn't find one and, steeling himself to it turned the woman over.

The sight turned his stomach. She was unrecognizable, just a piece of carved meat. Only Apaches could have used their knives so mercilessly and with such cruel, twisted imagination. He staggered away from the body as though it was an unclean thing, not wanting to think, just to get out of there.

The man lying motionless at the back of the building, an arrow protruding between his shoulder blades, forestalled that desire to run. At first, Gannon thought it inevitable he was dead, but the man's leg twitched and he forced himself to go and look. As he leaned over him, he could see his face was badly burned and could smell cooked flesh. A flap of skin was flopping over his forehead, the legacy of an aborted attempt at scalping. It was clear he wasn't going to survive much longer but, below that careless flap of flesh, two eyes like blue stones fixed on Gannon's face with a magnetic intensity. Miraculously his red-raw lips mouthed the word ... water.

Gannon responded by hurrying back to his horse with a bad feeling in his belly, as though a worm had been disturbed and was gnawing at his innards. His hand was shaking as he carried his canteen back to the dying man and knelt beside him again.

The man licked at the dribble of water Gannon administered to his desiccated lips. As though the liquid was some kind of magic elixir, he responded by trying to turn on to his side but fell back again. A second time he tried and this time Gannon placed a hand beneath his neck to support him. Seeing him fight so piteously for his life was heartbreaking.

'Give it up, feller,' Gannon said hoarsely. 'Just let go. Make it easy on yourself.'

The man's eyes widened, dragging Gannon in, commanding him to pay him due notice with the force of the will that lurked there. His lips started to work, and managed to form words, but Gannon had to lean close to hear them.

'Small barn,' he whispered, adding, in a voice like a low wind rustling through a dry brush, 'look . . . there.'

Gannon glanced over his shoulder and noticed a small barn which stood a little way off the main house. For some reason, probably because they figured the sparks would catch it anyway and set it alight, the intruders hadn't fired it. When his gaze returned, the rancher's eyes were shut but his lips were working furiously, like an automatic machine that churns away without producing the desired product.

'What?' Gannon said, moved by his struggle.

The eyes flew wide open once again but this time their blue stones had life in them, were brimming with a hatred drawn from as deep a well as man could reach into, that place where aeons of civilization counted for nothing because in its depths lay wild, primitive, animal instinct. Simultaneously, the ruins of his hands grasped at Gannon's shirt but couldn't find purchase.

'Drunk . . . Apache . . . bastards!' he yelled, his voice reaching for a crescendo which belied its former weakness with its ferocity.

Those were his last words, his last rail against the world and its cruelty. His hands fell away and his eyes lost all sensibility, turning back to stones as his body went limp. But his words, like a curse reverberating in the ether, swirled around Gannon. Then, like a bitter, icy wind their implication penetrated his essence with accusations.

He reached for the arrow sticking out of the dead man's back, snapped off the shaft and examined it. The colours of the twine bindings confirmed beyond doubt what he already suspected and dreaded: it was a Chiricahua war arrow. That meant only one thing: five of Chato's men had carried out the raid and, judging by the rancher's dying imprecation, they'd been fuelled by the liquor he and Mendoza had sold them.

Wanting to disbelieve but unable to deny the evidence, he rose to his feet. Assailed by his conscience and vaguely remembering the man's dying plea, he made for the barn as though in a dream. When he reached it, he gave way to the anger and guilt building inside him and kicked the doors open.

For a while, in the dim light, he could see nothing but could hear something, a faint noise that sounded like a cat mewing. Yet there was a piteous quality to the sound that reminded him of a wild animal too long caught in a trap, which has exhausted itself struggling until all that remains of its strength is in its vocal cords. Tracing the sound to its source, he focused on what at first glance seemed an amorphous shape hanging from one of the walls. Then, gradually, as his eyes grew accustomed to the poor light, the shape took on something like a human form. Finally and horrifically, he discerned it was a human child suspended there.

Like a piece of meat hung up to dry out, a little girl was hanging from a metal hook. The hook had pierced the flesh on the back of her neck the sharp upward curve of the hook emerging there like a grotesque, diabolic horn. The head framed in golden curls, was hanging low. Mercifully, she was in a state of delirium as she hung on to what remained of her life by a tenuous thread.

Gannon, overwhelmed by a surfeit of guilt, cried out in anguish. Somehow he managed to move himself and lift the girl off the hook, tearing her flesh as he manoeuvred her body, knowing even in his state of torment there was no easy way to do it that wouldn't add to her already unbearable pain. She screamed once, loud, then collapsed into his arms. As he carried her to the door he could feel warm liquid running down his cheek; he realized it was blood from her wounds pouring over him, the man responsible, in part at least, for its spilling.

Once outside in the light, and looking into the innocent face that had hardly yet begun its voyage into life, he was demented. The child's eyelids, as delicate as butterfly wings, were flickering; at any moment she might reawaken into her world of pain. Already she'd lost too much blood, suffered too much shock to survive and he knew that, ultimately, her brave fight for life could only end one way.

He willed her just to die but her eyes were opening and closing as she fought against the inevitable. Paralysed into inaction because there was nothing in the world he could do to change things, he just stood there holding her in his arms. Finally, in his torment, he did the only thing left and began to pray earnestly to God to spare her any more hurting.

When she still did not die, he knew it was down to him. Gently, he lowered her to the ground and slid his Peacemaker from his holster. His hand was shaking as he placed the pointed barrel against her temple. For a long time he just remained like that, willing himself to it. Then, screwing his eyes shut, he squeezed the trigger.

He heard the gun boom, felt the recoil and reluctantly opened his eyes. Like a discarded ragdoll, the child was lying at his feet, all signs of life gone. Momentarily, he experienced a sense of relief that it was all over for her at last, but it was a fleeting consolation as his guilt resurfaced and suffused as though a dam inside him had broken.

With cracking sounds like gunshots, the main building collapsed. He turned instinctively as the flames, like wild, red dancers, reached the climax of their act. In his state of mind, it was as though they had risen from hell's inferno itself, to mock him with a celebratory dance of death. All he wanted to do was to get as far away as he could from that place, and go somewhere he could forget what he had just witnessed. Yet, in his heart of hearts, he knew he would never be able to forget.

Without bothering to glance at the bodies he was leaving behind, he stumbled to his horse and threw himself on to its back. He smacked the animal's rump hard and it took off at a gallop. Gannon just let it have its head, not caring where it took him because he couldn't think of anywhere to run, and didn't think it would make much difference anyway, not now.

He camped that evening somewhere in the hills. In the morning, after a night of torment such as he'd never known, he walked like a zombie to the edge of a ravine. He took his share of the gold coins with him, and spilled them on to his open palm. Cursing his Maker, he drew back his arm and flung them over the edge to scatter far and wide, wishing he could so easily rid himself of the guilt they had brought him.

4

Ramirez's eyes narrowed as he withdrew into the shadows. He was halfway up the canyon side watching the Apache horsemen edging their way unsuspectingly along the narrow trail below. He considered God must be smiling on him, bringing him this gift. Aside from financial motivation, like many of his fellow Mexicans, he hated Apaches.

When they were closer, he saw they were Chiricahua, part of Chato's bunch. They'd been off the resevation for months now, raiding back and forth across the border. Careful not to move a muscle, he calculated how much money the government would pay for their scalps, and for so little effort. Of course, the blond-haired boy who rode in line behind the third Apache was an imponderable. Certainly no way could his scalp, bright yellow in the sun, be taken for an Indian's. Maybe he'd sell him as a slave. But if he proved too much trouble, maybe he'd just kill him. If he went down in the imminent fusillade, it would not matter much either. One more dead, gringo brat was all.

When they were far enough along the trail to make it difficult for their ponies to turn, Ramirez shouldered his rifle and drew a bead on the lead rider. He knew that his men, hidden like him, would follow his example and would pick out their agreed targets. It gave him much satisfaction that the Apaches, masters of the ambush themselves, were about to receive some of their own medicine.

When it was too late to matter, the lead Apache raised his hand tentatively. He was close enough for Ramirez to see his wide nostrils twitch and the *bandido* knew he'd caught their scent. The Indian lifted his head and scanned the rocks with a quick, turkey-like movement of his neck. Then he turned to warn his followers. Ramirez heard him say something sharply before he squeezed the trigger. His bullet took the Apache between the eyes, knocking him off his pony. The other Mexicans followed his lead and opened fire. The horsemen, unable to turn and run on the narrow trail, spilled from their horses like birds at a target shoot.

The crackle of the rifles gave way to silence. Only the boy remained astride his pony, and he was struggling with the frightened animal. One of the Mexicans broke cover, pulled him off its back and threw him on the ground where he lay half-stunned.

The Mexicans emerged and walked amongst the dead Apaches. While one of them calmed the riderless horses, the others drew their knives and set to the scalping with the economic movements of men who had perforned the task enough times for it to become automatic, a part of their trade.

Through half-closed eyes, as though he was awaking from a dream, the boy watched. Then, when his head started to clear and his vision sharpened, the carnage, the blood and the hideous scalpless heads convinced him this was no dream. His Apache captors had scared him enough but what he'd just seen the Mexicans perform was horrifying.

Ramirez at last turned his attention to the boy, seeing his shocked, bemused expression. Laughing, he strode over to where he lay, squatted in front of him and held a bloodied scalp a few inches from his face. He held out a hand and touched his yellow hair.

'You pretty lucky kid,' he said showing his black teeth, his narrow pig eyes scanning the boy's features. 'If your hair was black, Ramirez would kill you for your scalp. Maybe he kill you anyway. Could be, for you, Apaches not so bad as Ramirez.'

The boy said nothing. He had been taught to look people straight in the eye and that was what he did now. It seemed to disconcert the Mexican.

'What will you do with the gringo cur?'

One of his men, standing behind Ramirez, asked the question.

Ramirez tied the scalp to his belt and drew his knife. 'Best to kill him,' he said. 'Something about this gringo kid, I don't like.'

He grabbed the boy's shoulder, turned him round brought the blade against his throat.

'*Un momento,* Ramirez!'

Keeping the knife poised, ready to cut, the bandit leader looked round at the man who had interrupted.

'What is it Diego? You're keeping this gringo kid waiting. I think he might wet his pants.'

Diego, like his *compadres*, laughed ingratiatingly, then explained. 'I think I have seen this kid in Tucson. His father owns a store . . . *muchos pesos.* Perhaps he'd pay well for his kid. It would be a pity to kill him if that is so, huh?'

'His father is very rich?' Ramirez eased the blade away from the boy's neck as he asked.

'I think,' Diego said.

Ramirez lowered the knife, jerked the boy's head around to face him.

'Your father is rich man. Yes, kid?'

The boy's eyes met the Mexican's, and again did not drop away under their callous, calculating scrutiny. He nodded his head.

Ramirez reflected for a moment, then pushed him roughly away.

'We'll send a message to Tucson,' he announced.

Gannon was sitting in the dust, back against an adobe wall, upper body slouched forward, head hanging loose like a doll's. His poncho was dirty and the big sombrero, once white and now a deep shade of grey, hid his head and features completely. Around his neck a canteen hung loose. Nobody, at that moment, could have guessed he wasn't Mexican, though the people of the village knew it since he'd been moping around there for weeks, mostly in a drunken stupor.

The villagers were friendly, peaceable folk and the gringo had done them no harm. Being religious people, they considered it an unholy thing that the man called Gannon seemed to wish to drink himself to death. Shy to approach him themselves, they'd asked their priest to speak to him and, though a relationship of a kind had developed between the two men, there had been no let up in the amount of tequila and mescal the gringo consumed. It seemed the devil had him in his grip and would not let go. Even now, there was a bottle in his hand.

Gannon was lamenting that there were only a few drops of solace left in that bottle. His mind was still alert enough to realize that he had nothing left; the holster under his poncho was empty because he'd sold his gun, and his horse had gone long ago. All he had was what he was wearing and he realized his clothes were all that separated him from the dogs which, sensing his otherness in this village, would occasionally chase him in the street.

He was thinking of the woman. How long ago had it been? He was coming up forty now, and guessed it must have been all of twelve years ago when he'd left her. She'd foreseen this day, warning him he'd come to nothing if he continued his wild ways. His restlessness, that urge to keep moving, had driven him to leave her and now he'd done things which were coming back to haunt him.

Months of degradation had passed since he'd put the little girl out of her misery. He'd thought of going back to Tucson to try to find the woman and ask her forgiveness. Maybe she'd even give him another chance. But he knew deep down it was all too long ago, too much would have changed; once a hand was played, you couldn't retract it. He'd never given a man a second chance so did he deserve forgiveness? He thought not.

His reverie was broken by the drumming of hooves in the distance. When he looked up, he saw riders coming into the village at a gallop and noticed the villagers retreating into doorways. He tried to get up, fell back again, then decided he was better where he was. Who would look the way of a two-bit saddle bum who hadn't bathed in weeks? Instead, he took another long swig from the bottle.

From under the brim of his sombrero, he tried to focus as the riders pulled up in front of the low adobe building across the street which served as a *cantina.* He could see they were Mexicans, had ridden hard and seemed in a hurry for a drink. Then he noticed Apache scalps hanging from a saddle, and knew that these men were practitioners of a dirty trade – government sanctioned, scalps for dollars. He lowered his head again. For sure, there was nothing left for those scavengers to take from him. He figured they would see that at a glance and not disturb him.

'Tie the boy!' The command carried to Gannon from across the street but he wasn't curious.

Moments later hearing the jingle of spurs coming closer, he raised his head wearily. One of the Mexicans was dragging a fair skinned, yellow-haired boy across to the hitching rail close to where he was sprawled. He kept his head low and, when he raised it again, the boy's hands were tied to the rail, the Mexican walking back across the street. The kid's blue eyes met his own, equally blue. He saw a spark of defiance there, in spite of what had clearly been a rough time. He felt sympathy for the kid but he'd learned to mind his business. Even if he was armed, in a fit state to do anything about it, he knew he wouldn't; he had enough troubles. Lowering his eyes, he allowed his now customary lassitude to wash over him again.

'Will you help me mister?' The whispered words carried to him. He heard them but did not look up.

'Trouble helping myself, kid. Ain't got no gun and hardly got the legs to stand.' He paused, added, 'Don't feel too hard-done-by though. By the looks of things you're better off than those Apaches I'm guessing they took you from. You'll live.'

There was silence for a moment, then the boy spoke again, his voice weaker. 'I'm thirsty mister. At least let me have water.'

Gannon guessed that was a bothersome but reasonable request. It couldn't do either of them any harm, and a glance across the street told him all the Mexicans were inside. With an effort, using the adobe wall as a support, he slid his way up on to his feet and unslung the canteen from his shoulder. When he straightened and lurched towards the hitching rail he was clearly too tall and too light-skinned for a native of the country.

'Not too much,' he told the kid, handing him his canteen. 'Too much, too soon and you'll be sicker than a dog.'

The kid took his advice, drank slow, then handed the canteen back.

'Obliged,' he muttered.

Gannon turned away and started back. He froze mid-motion when the shot rang out lifting a cloud of dust in front of him. Cursing his luck, he leant against the wall as a voice snarled, 'Stay right there, gringo.'

He held his hands in the air, put his back against the wall and, like a shot animal going slowly to ground, slid resignedly to earth. Inwardly, he was cursing his stupidity. He should have known not to get involved, especially unarmed and only part aware.

Four of them stood over him. As he focused on their faces, he could tell there wasn't much humanity left in these men. Their eyes had that deadness he knew well. They were men who survived on their wits; there weren't many other layers of sensibility beneath that crucial motivation.

'You come between men and their business, gringo,' the Mexican with the gun in his hand said, surveying him with contempt.

Gannon kept his eyes averted. 'No trouble. I gave the kid a little water is all.' He gestured at his empty bolster. 'I ain't even carrying.'

'We don't like gringos here, Ramirez,' another Mexican said, addressing the one with the gun. 'They are like flies. One comes and more come. This is our land. We are kings here.'

'Kill him,' a third said. 'He is a man alone.'

'No!' The kid who'd been listening quietly, spoke up. 'All he did was bring me water. He doesn't deserve. . . .'

Ramirez turned towards him, took two quick strides, and struck him with the back of his hand with force enough to drive him to his knees. As he turned back to Gannon, he saw the gringo's right hand twitch slightly, knowing that if he'd had a weapon he just might have pulled it at that moment. The Mexican guffawed, and decided it would be best to kill him. This village was his, Ramirez's domain. Like his *compadre* said, they didn't want gringos coming here and interfering with a good thing.

'I think you could once have been a dangerous *bandito* like Ramirez, mister,' he announced, but sarcastically. 'Such a man I would not like behind me when I leave this place. Better for you and me you die now.'

Ramirez's gun started to come up. It crossed Gannon's mind, even as he feared the imminent bullet, that maybe this was for the best, what he deserved, an end to his uselessness. He closed his eyes and saw a vision of the woman, floating up from somewhere out of his past. It seemed a comfort as he waited.

Nothing happened. He wondered if they were toying with him but when he opened one eye he saw they were looking down the street. The priest was striding towards them, his black robes trailing behind him, a hand raised in protest. He halted in front of them, grey hair tousled, the deep tan of his middle-aged, benign face glistening with a sheen of sweat.

'What is this?' he said. 'I thought we agreed there'd be no killing here. That is why we give you food and drink. You say you protect the people.'

Ramirez glared at the priest. 'This man is not one of our people.'

'He is a guest,' the priest answered, glancing at the

boy now, noticing the tied hands. 'He is harmless, a man down on his luck. If you leave him be the people will call you merciful, they will respect you for it.'

Ramirez was quiet for a moment. He was a wily one this priest, a man who could play with words, but perhaps what he was saying made sense. The people here were afraid of him but he had never murdered any of them, merely used their food and tequila. There was a line and if he crossed it they might rise against him. And this priest was a cunning one. He had influence here. Maybe this time he should play the merciful one.

'*Sí*,' he said, holstering his gun. 'I will be merciful, let the gringo live. but if he is here when I return I will kill him. That is a promise, priest.'

The *bandito* turned away and gestured for his men to follow. But the priest wasn't finished. His eyes were on the boy.

'It would be seen as even more merciful if you left the boy.'

'Don't push too much, priest.' Ramirez called over his shoulder. 'The boy is business.'

One of the *banditos* cut the rawhide which bound the youngster and dragged him away after the others. The priest watched and Gannon, reading his features, saw the contained rage, the struggle for composure beneath the surface.

'Thanks,' he muttered.

The priest dragged his eyes from the boy and his captors, and looked down at Gannon.

'You and I are alike,' he said, self-contempt in his voice. 'You left your better self somewhere and me, well,

I didn't have the courage to stand up for that boy.'

'You did all you could,' Gannon said.

The priest shook his head. 'I was afraid, afraid for my own life if I pushed it.'

'Seems natural enough. They ain't exactly Sunday School teachers.'

The priest fingered the cross hanging round his neck as his eyes scanned the buildings where he knew the villagers would be watching.

'The people look to me. I am an example and yet I have let Ramirez ride away with a child. I have allowed him too much, averted my eyes too many times and now he has brought his evil into our midst for all to see.'

'Probably they'll sell the kid. He'll live at least.' Gannon said consolingly.

'Not the point,' the priest snapped at him. Then, he said more softly, 'As for yourself, you will have to leave. If you are here when they return there will be trouble for all of us.'

'I have no horse,' Gannon said.

'I will give you a mule.'

'I have no money, no gun, nowhere to go.'

'You will have as much as Jesus when he rode into Jerusalem.'

Gannon gave a wry smile. 'And look what happened to him.'

'You add blasphemy to your sins,' the priest told him. 'Maybe you should try to find that woman you talked about. Sometimes even the worst of us are given a second chance.'

With that parting shot he walked away, Gannon

watching with a mixture of emotions. The man had talked patiently with him many times, had listened to his drunken accounts of his misspent life with compassion, though he had never been able to bring himself to discuss the little girl and her family. He was sorry the priest was facing a crisis. A part of him wished he could have helped and gone up against those bandits, but he figured that part of him was too far gone to ever resurrect itself. Looking after himself was hard enough, and had become all he could manage.

When the *banditos* rode out, he had resumed his position against the wall. The boy sat astride a pinto and looked at Gannon from across the street but there was no appeal in his eyes. Instead he looked resigned, as though he was watching a chance disappear, regretting what might have been. Something in Gannon stirred, but it was far away, too deep inside to surface and he let it drain away with the tequila he poured into his throat.

5

'Gannon.'

The voice was familiar, but his head was aching so he turned over and ignored it. A moment later he felt something cold and disgusting press against his cheek and his eyes sprang open just as a long, coarse tongue licked his face. He rolled away in the straw and looked up into the grey face of the mule whose tongue had caressed him. The priest was watching with some amusment. He was holding another mule and both mules were packed. Behind him the stable doors were open, letting the sun in.

'Can you follow sign?' the priest asked. 'Show me where they went?'

Gannon's befuddled mind gradually shaped the previous day's events. His eyebrows rose in wonderment.

'Give it up, Father. You can do nothing for the boy, especially in their own backyard. They will kill you.'

'I will try,' the priest said, simply. 'I do not ask more than to know where their camp is. You can leave me then.'

Gannon rose, stretched to his full height, walked outside and submerged his head in the water trough. When he emerged, he ran his fingers through his long blond hair and shook off the moisture as the priest stood behind him, watching expectantly. He knew he had to leave anyway and he was used to the territory. He figured he could do what the priest asked and go his own way.

'You know I can't pay for the mule?'

'I do not ask. Leave me when we are near their camp. Head over the border, back to your own kind. Try to find the woman. She may even need you.'

'More like she's married with six kids,' Gannon said wryly, feeling foolish for having told the priest so much about himself. He should have buried the past, not let the drink and his depression revive it. It had all been so long ago, hadn't it?

'At least you could make your peace with her. I know your conscience is troubling you.'

Gannon studied the priest as he thought the matter through. The woman was just one thing he had on his conscience. He knew shame and a minuscule amount of pride would not let him seek her out. Maybe he'd go back to Tucson though, for a while, then just keep riding until fate played him another hand. It was the way he had lived before Yuma Prison. Probably the mould was set hard and he was too old to change. If he kept moving he might forget what he'd become, leave it behind. He thought about trying to change the priest's mind for his own good but thought better of it; he was probably the last person he would listen to.

'I can read sign,' he said, deciding. 'I will take you so far on your fool's errand since you are generous with the mule.'

The priest handed him the reins of the same animal that had rudely awakened him. He took Gannon's canteen and his own to the trough and filled them. Then he mounted and gestured to Gannon to climb on to his own mule.

'We're agreed,' he said, his face set hard. 'So let's get going.'

Gannon mounted, feeling he cut a foolish figure as his long legs almost touched the ground. The incongruous pair – the man of God and the boozed up saddle-tramp – rode out side by side, into the bare landscape which gave way to the serrated peaks of the Sierra Madre mountains on the horizon.

Ramirez and his men had left clear tracks across the flat scrubland. Gannon had no problem following, rarely having to stop. He figured the *bandito* must be pretty confident to leave such clear sign. The main problem was the the slow progress of the mules and the blazing sun. Several times they had to drink some of their precious water.

It was a relief to reach the foothills in the late afternoon and manoeuvre the animals into the shade of the giant rocks whenever the chance presented itself. Gannon became more cautious now, since on the bare rock the sign wasn't so clear and he was aware that Apaches sometimes passed this way. From the freshness of the tracks, he figured they were not too far behind but, as the light began to fade, he decided it would probably be the next day before they caught up and it would be best to set up camp for the night.

'Look!'

The priest paused mid-action as he was handing Gannon a blanket. His free arm rose and pointed. Gannon's eyes followed its direction.

'Can't see nothing,' he muttered, squinting into the darkness.

'There was a flash of light up there.'

'I thought it was me liked the booze,' Gannon muttered, starting to turn away.

'There!' the priest said.

This time Gannon saw it too, a flicker of light against the encroaching darkness. It had been no more enduring than a flaring match in a cupped hand. He knew the light came from a fire, and they watched in silence for several minutes though it did not show again. Gannon was disturbed because it seemed so close. Maybe he'd miscalculated and Ramirez was nearer than he thought. In these parts such an error could cost you dear, and he wondered if the copious amounts of alcohol with which he'd punished his body had impaired his judgement.

The priest watched as he climbed wearily on to the mule once again. He started up himself but Gannon motioned to him dissuasively.

'I need a close look,' he said. 'You rest here until I'm back.'

'You think it's Ramirez?'

'Better to find out,' Gannon said kicking the mule's haunches. 'Hope it's him, not Apaches.'

'God go with you,' the priest whispered as the night swallowed man and mule. He settled down to await their return, wrestling with his fear of what might lie ahead, hoping his nerve and faith would hold if his plans went awry.

For an hour he sat, waiting for Gannon to return. It crossed his mind that the man could just have taken off into the night leaving him there. But the doubt was momentary. In spite of all Gannon had told him about his past, he somehow had faith in him to keep his word.

That faith was justified a little later when Gannon rode in. Without saying anything he dismounted, tethered the mule and squatted beside the priest.

'It's them all right.' His voice was a little shaky because their proximity had surprised him. 'Half a mile up. They're in a circle of rocks.'

The priest sighed, like a man resigning himself to an illness from which he might never recover. He lifted his head to the heavens and his lips moved wordlessly. When he'd finished, he laid a hand on Gannon's shoulder.

'You've kept your part of the deal. Now get out of here.'

Gannon hesitated. 'In the morning,' he mumbled. 'You can go to their camp in the morning when I leave.'

'Go now!' the priest ordered, his tone implacable. 'You've kept your bargain and I want you gone from here.'

'It won't make no difference if—'

'Now,' the priest repeated, more gently. 'I don't want them to know you were on their trail. That will make it worse for me. The sooner you're gone the better.'

Gannon saw some sense in that. He didn't want them to know either. They would kill him without a thought out here.

'You aiming to tell them you got here by a miracle, that God brought you to them.'

'Maybe he did. Maybe he chose you. Whichever, some of those men are superstitious. Wondering how I found them will give them something to think about.'

Gannon rose from his haunches. He was thinking it made no difference to him. What the priest said made sense. He figured Ramirez would not give up the boy anyway, that the priest was on a fool's errand. From what he knew of the Mexican mentality, more than likely they would send him back because he was no threat and they would be superstitious about harming priests.

'Good luck, then,' he said and mounted up again. 'Thanks for the mule and the advice, Father.'

Once again, he rode away into the night. This time he was thinking he would put distance between himself and Ramirez then get some shuteye. Thanks to the gift of the mule he was at least mobile again and, from his recent perspective, that was at least a step up in the world. Yet though he tried to forget what was behind him and think ahead, his mind periodically returned to the priest and what he was trying to do for the captive boy. The priest had guts, he had to give him that, and he hoped the worst that could happen would be that Ramirez would laugh at him and send him back with his tail between his legs.

As he prepared himself to move out, the priest's line of thought was contradictory to Gannon's. He knew the hearts of men well enough, and had already anticipated that the *banditos* would be impervious to any plea from him. It would indeed take a miracle, as Gannon had suggested, to talk the boy away from them, especially in their own domain. It would take action, not words. He hoped God would forgive him for not believing he could appeal to the good in Ramirez and that, when he tried to rescue the boy, the good Lord would not desert him. And if his life was to be forfeit in the process, he hoped his courage would not fail him.

His hood covering his head, he worked his way up to their camp and studied the layout, hardly believing the *banditos* were so careless. As far as he could see, only one of the men was awake. He was sitting apart from the rest watching the horses and facing away from the camp. The boy lay with the men, distinguishable because, unlike the rest, no sombrero covered his head and his frame was much smaller. If only the guard remained where he was, perhaps there was a chance.

With a silent prayer he rose and started in, his long robe and hood a perfect camouflage, blending him with the darkness. He expected only in the circle would he be seen clearly, but he didn't plan to linger there. The old pistol he'd secreted under his robe made him uncomfortable. He intended to use it only as a last resort and then as a threat rather than a killing tool. But it didn't fit with his calling, and his unease about it grew as he neared the circle.

His eyes riveted on the guard's back, willing him not to turn. As though it was a holy place he was entering in reverential silence, he shuffled his sandals across the soft sand, headed for where the boy lay. Close now, he could see the yellow hair flowing, spilling over the top of the blanket. The persistent cacophony of snoring was a comfort as the distance closed, for it meant they had not seen him enter. If his luck held . . . .

Finally he bent, pulled the blanket back and thrust his hand over the boy's mouth. He felt the youngster's body tense as he awakened and looked up at the hooded head hovering over him. He put a warning finger to his lips. If the boy made a noise now it would be finished. He hoped, in the dim light and coming out of sleep, he wouldn't panic but quickly assess he was there to help him.

The boy's tentative smile, as he removed his hand from his mouth, reassured him. He helped the youngster to his feet. In one swift movement, he used the knife he was carrying under his robe to slash the rope around his wrists. Then, like a fussy mother marshalling one of her brood, he started to manoeuvre the boy across the clearing. With each step his spine tingled with dread of discovery, and each grunt from a slumbering Mexican was magnified into a roar aimed in their direction.

They were going to make it – the priest was sure of it. They'd reached the fringes of the sleeping figures; the cover of the rocks was only yards away now. Beyond that, the gigantic cloak of darkness was ready to absorb them. God was helping. They were so near. Another moment and—

'*Madre de Cristo*!'

Three blasphemous words, which on his own lips would have been a blessing, seemed to mock him as they blasted into the night, fracturing hope.

The man rose from his blankets. He was so close the priest could smell him and his great featureless mass seemed inhuman as he blocked their way, like a guardian of an evil place somewhere between this existence and the next. The priest saw his arm rise, seeing the flash of silvery metal as the knife reached its zenith. In the second before it plunged, he withdrew the old gun from under his robe, took desultory aim and jerked the trigger. Even as the weapon exploded, he whispered a prayer for forgiveness.

Time seemed to freeze. The *bandito* hovered, knife arm poised above his head as though held there by an invisible force, the priest motionless with shock. Then the scene unfroze and as he fell, the Mexican thrust down with the last of his strength. The knife pierced the black robes and plunged into flesh close to the heart.

The holy man felt the pain as the knife went in and knew he was finished. With the remnants of his will he stayed upright, and as the rest of the camp came alive, he thrust the gun into the boy's hands.

'Run!' he gasped, fighting for the words. 'I'm dying.'

His voice seemed to him a disembodied, strangulated imitation of what it had been. As he toppled, he saw the boy had not obeyed it, and was looking bewildered. He hit the ground hard, swallowing sand and dirt. One last time through blurred vision, he looked up, distraught that the youngster seemed rooted to the spot.

'Go!' he yelled, before a coughing spasm overtook him.

This time the youngster seemed to understand, and the priest was relieved to see him turn and run. His last prayer, before his spirit left him, was for the boy: that God would protect him and send him safely home.

Fear drove the boy on. He ran blindly, knowing only that he wanted to be as far from that place as possible. Time and time again he stumbled against rocks, and tore his skin on prickly cacti. But the pain was nothing compared to his desire to escape, which was mixed with sadness that the priest had given his life for him. Somehow, he sensed the holy man would not like it if his sacrifice was in vain and that thought gave him extra determination.

When he could run no more, he dived into a rock crevice and lay listening, his breathing resounding in his ears until he was sure the *banditos* would hear it. When it had evened out, instinct and fear told him to get up and run again but intelligence overcame compulsion. They could be close, watching for movement. Better to lie there, like an animal gone to ground in its lair. The darkness was his best ally if he lay still. There wasn't much moonlight; it would be difficult to track him. He would wait.

He heard two voices coming closer, and gripped the old pistol which he'd placed in his belt. Peering out into the night, shivering because the air had turned cold, he spotted them ten yards off, standing together. Others soon joined them, black shadows converging out of the night.

'This is foolish,' he heard one say. 'We cannot track in the dark.'

'Best we wait until tomorrow,' another chipped in. 'He is only a kid. He will run himself out. Tomorrow we will use our horses. It will be easy.'

'Let us return,' a third said. 'We will tell Ramirez that tomorrow we can be certain. Why lose sleep? How far can the kid get on foot? One or two of us could fetch him when the sun rises.'

Relieved, the boy watched them turn back. Yet his spirits were dampened for they had spoken the bare truth. How long would he be able to evade them? He was alone in a harsh land. The *banditos* were expert trackers. Tomorrow he would be the fly to their spider. And even if he kept running, somehow escaped them, how would he survive. . . ? He could perhaps get water from cacti, maybe find a spring . . . kill for meat.

A wave of depression hit him after the euphoria of his freedom. The reality was he had no chance. Better to just lie there and let them find him in the morning than pit himself against those men, this savage land. What was the point? Then he remembered the priest who had been so brave and thought, too, of his parents worrying about him back in Tucson and he knew he had to try. Resolved to give it his best go, he crawled out and started to run again.

He had not gone far when he glimpsed a dark shape standing motionless ahead. Fingers touching the gun in his belt he went into a crouch, fearing it was a cougar on the prowl, that it would smell the blood from his cuts. But, when he risked another look, he realized it was too big for a cougar, and recognized the shape as a mule's, tethered and grazing on galleta grass. He circled the animal warily, his eyes everywhere, but could find no sign of a camp. Then he realized the mule was probably the priest's, left behind when he'd started in. His spirits lifted again. It was not a horse to outrun his pursuers, but it would give him some distance and maybe the providence which had helped him this far would be generous again.

He approached the animal whispering reassurances. It did not resist when he caressed its long nose, nor when he untethered it and climbed on to its back. He looked up at the sky, read the stars as his mother had taught him to do, then headed in a northerly direction. He thought he might now have a small chance.

7

Gannon was standing in the head-tall, manzanita grass holding the mule back because it was eager to get to the water. He had been there a long time, watching the spring up ahead, ascertaining there was no movement before he moved in. One more refill for his canteen and he figured he wouldn't have to risk stopping again. Water out here was a precious commodity and a place like this, which attracted all kinds of varmints, was best avoided if you could – especially if you were unarmed. Once again, he wondered why he'd been foolish enough not to ask the priest for a weapon. It was the omission of a crazy man. What had he been thinking?

He made up his mind to move, glanced at his back trail one more time, and saw a lone rider emerge from an *arroyo* on to the flat-sanded approaches to the water. He withdrew further into the manzanita. His first thought was Apache and he cursed his luck. There was nothing he could do about it though. He was stuck there; he'd just have to bide his time, wait until the rider was finished at the waterhole.

But the rider approached with a careless disregard for safety and when he was nearer Gannon recognized the yellow hair. It was the boy, Ramirez's captive, astride the priest's mule. He looked exhausted. But where was the priest? He waited until he had ridden past then stepped out and spoke sharply.

'That's the priest's mule you're riding, boy.'

The boy whirled, nearly coming off the animal's back as he came out of a half-sleep, but managed to pull the pistol and point it. Gannon raised his hands, his gaze taking in the boy's matted hair, heavy-lidded eyes and the cuts on his arms and legs.

'Don't you remember me boy, back at the village?'

The boy squinted against the sun. Gannon could see he was drained, that he needed water desperately, and figured his mule must have smelled it up ahead and carried him here.

'I remember,' the boy muttered, lowering the gun.

'Where's the priest? He was going to get you.'

'He died getting me free,' the boy said, his voice hoarse sounding from taut nerves and a parched throat. He looked towards his back trail. 'There's two of Ramirez's men not far behind. Seen 'em last time I stopped.'

Gannon wiped his brow with his kerchief. He didn't need this complication. All he wanted was to cross the border and get out of Mexico in peace. That old priest had been a stubborn cuss but he'd had plenty of guts and he was sorry he'd died. But it would have been better if he'd let the *banditos* keep the boy, because now he'd landed Gannon in a tight spot too and he'd had his fill of trouble.

'You sure there's only two of 'em boy?'

'Sure and they ain't far behind, mister.'

He studied the boy who was looking increasingly unsteady. Deciding there was no choice now, he formed a crude plan.

'You got to give me that gun, boy, then ride in to that waterhole, drink your fill and make as if you're all done in, which shouldn't be too hard seeing as you are.'

The boy gave him a distrustful look, his blue eyes wary. Gannon knew he was remembering his inertia back at the village, wondering how far he could trust this saddle bum.

'They pick up my tracks, they might get curious about me too,' he added to allay the youngster's fears. 'We're in this one together. Besides, state you're in you've no choice. On this one you got no options. Got to trust me.'

The youngster took only a moment to decide that was the truth of it. But there was still reluctance and suspicion in his eyes as he handed over the gun and with one last, doubtful glance at the man to whom he was entrusting his future, he spurred the mule ahead.

'Remember to act confused, like the sun got you,' Gannon called after him as he checked the gun's chamber and slid it into his holster before stepping back into the grass.

He waited there a good hour, getting thirstier. Time dragged, testing his patience, and he began to wonder if the boy had deluded himself, that in his weak state he'd imagined his pursuers. Then suddenly, they were there, edging their horses out of the *arroyo* from where the boy had come. One of them produced a spy glass, focusing it on the waterhole. After that they waited for some time, men and animals motionless. Finally, deciding there was no danger, they spurred their horses and rode flat out across the sand.

Gannon left his mule and started in after them, working his way through the grass. He took advantage of the cover it afforded until he reached clearer ground, where he sprinted in a crouching run between the scattered patches of mesquite, gun in hand, prepared for the *banditos* to spot him any moment and come charging up the slight declivity which led down to the spring. But he made it all right and flattened out in the sand.

In the shade of the few sparse cottonwoods, one of the Mexicans was tying the boy's wrists whilst the other slapped his face, berating him for costing them so much time and trouble. Gannon had to give the youngster his due: he was standing up to it, taking those blows without squealing which seemed to infuriate his tormentor even more.

He tried to shake off the weeks of drunken inertia, stealing himself to move in on them fast. Handling the unfamiliar gun didn't bother him; he knew how to use it better than most men. The only thing was, he'd been trying to avoid something like this. That's why he'd lingered in the village, hoping for a respite from his old ways. Drink had been his attempt to forget, assuage the conscience that had caught him up after all those years, driving him into a mental wilderness for which retreat from the world had seemed the only antidote. Now he was being forced by circumstance to emerge.

Before Ramirez had entered the equation the priest had tried to help him, convince him a man could change. The irony was that the priest's impracticality had put him right back here with a gun in his hand and the likelihood of more killing. He was half-tempted to just ride away but knew he couldn't get out of this one so easy. For some reason the priest's voice was still in his head, prodding him to finish what he'd started. He couldn't shake it off and, cursing the world, he leapt to his feet and started down on the Mexicans at a run.

He was upon them before they could react. The boy saw him first and broke away, while the Mexican who'd been manhandling him made a twitchy move for the gun on his hip, thought better of it, and glared at Gannon from under the brim of his sombrero. The other one took a half-step towards his horse but checked himself, his eyes flirting with the rifle in the saddle boot, not able to decide if the chance was worth courting. Finally, his eyes left it alone and blazed at Gannon instead.

'It's the gringo from the village,' he stated resentfully. He scratched his bulging stomach and spat into the sand.

'Ramirez will not like this and he is not so far away,' the other one said, nonchalantly smoothing down the moustache which dominated his face. 'What you want gringo?'

'The boy goes with me,' Gannon said. 'And you have a long walk ahead of you.'

The moustachioed *bandito* shook his head. 'My friend is too fat to walk.'

Gannon nodded knowingly. He understood. These two didn't rate him; they were going to go for it, take a chance against his gun because they feared returning to Ramirez without the boy.

'He is not worth it for you,' the fat one said, 'not worth your life.'

'It's me who's holding the gun,' Gannon said. 'Get out of here. while you can.'

His words trailed away as the fat one galvanized his bulk and started for the rifle. Gannon shot him in the shoulder. As the other took advantage and reached for his holster, Gannon's gun arm swivelled again. He fired twice. One bullet took the Mexican in the stomach, the other in the heart. Before he hit the ground, Gannon's gun hand was already swivelling back to the fat one.

Considering his corpulence and shoulder wound, the Mexican had moved with remarkable agility. He had managed to propel himself into the saddle, and was already urging the animal clear of the cottonwoods. But it was still an easy shot for Gannon as he levelled the gun at his back.

'*No*!'

Something slapped down on his arm, ruining the shot. Momentarily, he glared down at the boy who had spoiled his aim. Again he lifted his arm but this time the boy was pulling at his sleeve and the bullet whistled harmlessly over the fat man's head as he sped away. To compound Gannon's fury, the dead man's horse broke its tether and ran after the fleeing Mexican.

He snapped at the youngster. 'What in hell's teeth—'

'It is a bad thing,' the boy said, staring up at Gannon.

'What is?'

'To kill a man if you don't have to . . . and in the back.'

Gannon drew a breath, and stored his frustration.

'He is barely a man, and when he brings the others he will show us no mercy. Didn't you learn that when you were amongst them?'

'In the Bible. . . .'

'Ramirez knows the book boy. But it don't mean diddly to him nor any Apaches who might be wondering about those shots. Thanks to you, we got trouble.'

The boy's head was down. In spite of himself, Gannon started to feel sorry for him. He'd come through a lot. He remembered how he'd tried to defend him back in the village when the *banditos* were about to kill him.

'What's your name, boy?'

'James William Trueman,' the youngster answered warily, still wondering about Gannon's mood. 'But they call me Billy.'

'James, huh! Same name as me. Never brought me much luck. You did right to lose it. I'll call you Billy.'

'Are we still in trouble, mister?'

Gannon scanned the horizons, as though he wished he could levitate and see what lay beyond their limits.

'Depends on Ramirez's mood, or how much you're worth to him.'

The boy looked downcast as he muttered, 'He will come.'

'How can you be so sure?'

'My father has property in Tucson—'

Gannon interrupted him with a groan. 'So Ramirez intends to ransom you.'

The boy brushed his hair out of his eyes and squinted at Gannon. 'Can we get away?'

Gannon was already turning towards the manzanita grass where he'd tethered his mule.

'Fill the canteens, collect the weapons and get your mule ready,' he called over his shoulder. 'And maybe say a prayer, 'cos we might need some of that blind faith of yours before we're through.'

Gannon drove them all morning through canyons and valleys. He barely spoke to the boy and Billy reciprocated, sensing the man was concentrating hard on the trail. His eyes were everywhere, as though even the smallest feature of the landscape was a cause of speculation for him. He began to realize that alone he would have had no chance out here, that fate had brought him to this man and all his hopes were invested in him. Back in the village he'd disdained to help him, but at the waterhole he'd saved him. What manner of man was he? Perhaps the waterhole had been self-preservation, rather than any idea of helping; he'd said as much. If Ramirez was close, would Gannon see this business through or just leave him to his fate? He could not be sure.

The climbing got harder, the heat almost unbearable. Then around noon, the mules negotiated a narrow fissure and emerged on to a flat mesa. Gannon called a halt, gave the mules a little water from one canteen, then allowed himself and the boy a swig from the other. That done, with the boy following, he strode to the edge of the mesa and looked back.

Billy realized then why Gannon had made them climb. The view was magnificently all-embracing. He could see the waterhole they'd left that morning, the foothills and most of the trail they'd followed up into the mountains. When he turned to the man, he saw his gaze was fixed. Following its direction, he noticed the faintest movement of dust edging the foothills.

'Is it him?' Billy asked, trying to keep his voice even.

'Guess it is.'

'Will they catch up?'

Gannon thought about it. 'Touch and go. The mules are better'n horses up here but eventually we'll have to go down. It's a flat ran into Tucson. Better for horses. Judging distances, I'd say it's even money.'

'What about the Indians?'

'Got to take some chances, boy. We just got to be lucky. Ramirez will have to be careful too. Difference is, he's got enough guns to take risks.'

Gannon idled back to the animals. Billy couldn't understand why he wasn't hurrying. He figured the sight of those Mexicans should have put a burr under his saddle. Instead, the man found shade, and gestured for Billy to join him. He sat down beside him, puzzled at this casualness until Gannon explained.

'We rest an hour now. If we have to run on the flats, the mules will have a lot more left to give us. Plus, we'll be more alert. Can't afford not to be on the way down.'

A silence developed between them. Billy guessed the man, never vociferous, did not want to talk, and was surprised when he was first to break the silence.

'How'd you end up with Ramirez, kid?'

'He took me from the Apaches,' Billy answered, shivering involuntarily at the memory of the massacre. 'They scalped all the Indians.'

'How'd the Apaches get you, first off?'

Billy bit his lip, and looked guilty. 'I rode too far out of Tucson.'

'Your ma and pa let you go alone?'

'Naw, I snook off. Got a new horse and wanted to try him.' He reddened, ashamed of this misdemeanour and its consequences. My ma and pa won't know what happened to me. This Apache called Chato just came out of nowhere and took me.'

Gannon's head jerked back in reaction to the name. 'Ramirez killed Chato in that ambush huh?'

'Naw, he went ahead with others. They were taking me back to their camp.'

A lizard ran from under a rock, lay motionless near Gannon's feet, then scuttled off to find shade. They both watched it idly.

The boy said, 'My pa will reward you. He owns two stores and a stable.'

Gannon raised his eyebrows. 'Already got a reward in mind, boy, just like Ramirez has. That's why he'll keep on coming.'

'Then you are very much like Ramirez, mister, if you are helping me just for the reward.'

Gannon smirked at him. 'Your pa's a businessman, ain't he? Thought he would have taught you money makes the world turn.'

'My pa is a good man.' Billy's voice rose a decibel.

'He says money ain't everything. He says you don't judge a man by what he's got.'

Gannon laughed at him. 'Those that have it always say that, kid.'

'He worked for every penny. He did it for me and my ma. He had nothing when he came to Tucson.'

'Well, kid, he might be right back to nothing if Ramirez takes you and asks for that ransom. Me, I won't ask anything near as much, so you'd better hope it's me gets you back.'

There was silence between them again. The boy was wondering if the man was serious, if all that counted with him was money. He'd imagined he could see good in him but his words were contrary. Once again, he wasn't sure if, when it came to it, he could trust him, that in a tight spot he wouldn't think of his own survival and run.

'Think your pa will be out looking for you kid?'

Billy looked away at the horizon. 'Don't think so. Maybe he'll send men to look?'

It was said forlornly, as though he didn't want to pursue the matter, and seemed glad Gannon didn't press him. His pa would have gone looking if he could have done; he knew that. Even if he wasn't his real pa, he'd been as good as and he wouldn't swap him. He shut his eyes and when he opened them again the man was on his feet preparing the mules.

'Bet you wish you'd let me shoot that damned Mexican now, don't you boy?' he said as they mounted.

Billy bit his lip, shook his head. 'My pa says nothing's better than a clean conscience.'

Gannon cast his eyes downwards for a moment, then kicked his mule into action. Strangely, the boy felt he had hit a chord with Gannon, as though his answer had stirred a memory.

By late afternoon they'd made good progress. They were picking their way down a trail that led into a narrow canyon when the rifle shot echoed out. Gannon straightened, his features even more alert. When only silence followed, he grabbed the mules' reins and pulled them into the rocks beside the trail. Billy could tell he was more worried now than he'd seen him.

'That shot came from the bottom of the canyon where we're headed,' he told Billy.

The boy's eyes opened wide. 'They got ahead of us?'

'Couldn't have done. They must be behind. Didn't have time to get that far.'

The unspoken words hovered on the air, until the boy voiced them plaintively. 'You think they're Apaches?'

Gannon didn't answer the question, and just said, 'There's only two ways down for us. The canyon is one of them?'

'Where's the other?'

'Narrow trail further back, but it's longer and it would be risky to turn round when we don't know where Ramirez is. Best to take a look where that shot came from, see if we can still go through.'

Gannon grasped the rifle he'd acquired at the waterhole, tethered the mules, and beckoned the boy to follow. After a half hour of slow progress on a narrow, higher route that paralled the canyon's course, he halted pushed the boy flat. With Billy behind him he crawled to a vantage point.

Sweat pouring into Billy's eyes distorted his vision. At first, all he could make out were buzzards hanging on the air, occasionally swooping, then rising again to resume a watching brief. As his vision cleared, he noticed one bird became more daring, dropping lower. Following its flight, he spotted the focus of its attention. Across the trail below, men's bodies lay in grotesque postures, arrows protruding from torsos and limbs.

There had been a terrible slaughter here, As though the gesture could make the carnage disappear, Billy rubbed his eyes hard. But reality was still down there and, from where he was stationed, those cadavers seeemed as inanimate as the stern grey rocks around him. To him, it seemed nothing with a personality could ever have inhabited their bodies and made them men.

Nauseous, Billy glanced at Gannon for his reaction. The man was ceaselessly scanning the scene, taking everything in. When Billy looked back down, his focus sharpened and he caught a movement in a circle of rocks near where the bodies lay. He saw that two men armed with rifles were sheltering there, hugging the rocks. Recognizing one of them, he started to rise but Gannon pulled him down again.

'You crazy, boy?'

He tried to pull away but Gannon kept hold. 'Let me go,' he said. 'I know one of them.'

Gannon slapped his face hard; he recoiled with the shock.

'Get a grip, kid!' Gannon said. 'Take a better look. You'll live longer.'

Smarting from the blow and hurt pride, he did as he was bidden but he could see nothing, and didn't know what Gannon was talking about. Then, as he was about to give up, he noticed a brief flash of red against the grey rocks. Looking hard, he saw at first one, then several figures; they were hiding in the rocks below. The figures were focusing on the two men with rapt attention, like a pack of hunting dogs on invisible leashes, held back only by ancient instinct until a final moment of weakness in the ones they hunted. The long, black hair – worn loose and wild by some, in others partially restrained with bandannas – made them unmistakably Apache. With the recognition, a shiver coursed through Billy's body.

'Chiricahua,' Gannon muttered, disappointedly. 'Chato's bunch.'

Billy fought his tears. 'My pa must have sent men to find me. That man down there is a good friend of his.'

Narrowing his eyes, Gannon glanced up at the sun. 'We best pray this is over for them by sundown, and for our own sakes those 'paches are out of the canyon.'

'Can't we help those men?' There was an edge of desperation in the youngster's voice.

'That would be foolhardy. There's twenty of those devils. I'd maybe get one or two of 'em before the rest disappeared. Next time you'd see 'em, they'd be coming right at us.'

'We just going to watch?'

Gannon glanced at him scathingly. 'Nothing else we

can do, unless you want to end up buzzard meat like those fellers.'

He'd hardly finished speaking when shouting rose up from the canyon, and one of the Apaches stood up and threw a canteen on to the open ground close to where the men were sheltering. The gesture was accompanied by a rise in the volume of Apache voices, and it didn't take a translation to appreciate the wheedling tones, to know that they were baiting their enemy with the promise of water in the canteen, daring them to try for it.

'Don't think it'll be long now.' Gannon said.

Two minutes later, they saw one of the besieged men move. The other one grabbed his arm, only to be shaken off. The man who'd made the move burst out of the rocks, firing crazily at targets he could only be imagining as he sprinted the twenty yards to the canteen. He reached it without any impediment but, as his arm swept downwards, an Apache exploded from cover, a bolas whirling above his head. The white man had the canteen in his hand when the Apache released it with an expert flourish. It snaked through the air and the thongs entangled themselves round the man's ankles like tentacles. He managed to stagger a few steps before he unbalanced, and the moment he hit the dirt, two more Apaches broke cover. One dealt him a stunning blow with a war club and together they swept him up and, as though he were weightless, carried him into cover. The whole procedure was carried out with immaculate timing, and minimum risk.

'Why didn't they just kill him?' Billy said, shaken by what he had witnessed.

'We'll find out soon enough,' Gannon told him, a grim foreboding in his voice.

Those words proved true when screams rose from the canyon bottom, as though from the blackest pit of the world, a place where all pain gathered and transmogrified itself into a travesty of a human voice. They could not pinpoint its source until a bloodied creature, hardly a man anymore, crawled with painful slowness into the open. The creature had been stripped naked, half-skinned and they were shooting arrows into the body, deliberately avoiding the vital organs in order to prolong the agony.

Gannon and the boy listened to his screams as the shades of evening descended and the cliffs took on a purplish hue. Those twilight colours were beautiful on the mountain; another time they might have wondered at them. But the persistent screams were an ugly blemish on the face of nature so that neither man nor boy paid the slightest notice; they just wanted it to end.

Instead, as the last dregs of light were fading away, the man who was still sheltering in the rocks gave way, and started shouting gibberish at the encircling Indians. Finally, his nerve gone entirely, he stood away from his cover, put his gun to his head and pulled the trigger. The boy turned away as the man who had been his father's friend buckled at the knees and gave up the ghost.

Gannon saw the tears coursing down Billy's cheeks. He figured what they had just witnessed was hard enough on a man, never mind a kid. He searched for appropriate words.

'Some things you can do nothing about, no matter how much you hate them, Billy.'

'I wish I was home,' the boy sobbed.

'Well, this ain't home, but at least Ramirez ain't likely to come riding up with those Apaches around. Down side is, looks like those injuns are making camp for the night and we can't get through.'

Billy dried his tears on his sleeve, recovering his composure. 'What can we do about it?'

'Best we settle here. Come morning, if those Apaches are still down there, we'll try the other way down to the flats.'

Gannon left the boy alone while he went back to check on the mules and fetch blankets. Billy was not sure of the man who sometimes seemed cold-blooded and, at other times, to have a heart, and feared he might just run off and leave him, but he was back within an hour and they settled for the night higher up the mountain. Sleep did not come easy though, because he was conscious that not far below was the stuff of the worst possible nightmares. He soon sensed Gannon was awake as well.

'What were you doing in that Mexican village?' he asked in a whisper, to make conversation, but also to reassure himself about this man he did not really know and upon whom he was forced to depend.

'Running,' Gannon answered, with a yawn.

'Who from?'

There was a fraction's hesitation. 'Myself.'

It was a difficult concept for a youngster to grasp. 'Yourself?'

Gannon snorted. 'I've been a bad man, kid. I was trying to forget some of the things I done, one thing in particular. Then those *banditos* rode into my life. Trouble comes when I ain't even looking.'

'What was the bad thing you did?'

'Traded with some Apache a few months back, whiskey, mescal and other goods for gold coins. Next day some of the same bunch, drunk on mescal, rode on to a ranch and killed the whole family.' Gannon swallowed hard. 'They left the five year old daughter of the house alive but hung up on a hook.'

Billy could sense the man's pain and guilty conscience transcend even the darkness. 'What happened to her?'

'Never mind!' Gannon snapped, as though suddenly aware he'd said too much. 'Don't be telling anybody 'bout that either. Main thing is you know what kind of feller you're tied in with and how bad those varmints down there can be, if you aren't already convinced.'

Billy had already detected the turmoil in the man. Now he thought he knew its source. There was an aura of loneliness and sadness about him too.

'You got no family mister.'

Gannon laughed ironically. 'Nope. There was a woman I should have married but I let her down. Guess if we make it to Tucson and she's still around I'll call on her. The priest said I should ease my conscience by making my peace with her. After that I'll head for California, try to start again.'

There was a natural end to the conversation. Billy lay half-awake most of the night, turning over in his head what Gannon had told him. It sounded as though he was weary of his old life and genuinely regretful but, when it came right down to it, would he revert to his old self? Billy just couldn't decide and hoped such a choice would never present itself.

The morning brought disappointment. Gannon hoped the Apaches would be gone at sunrise but they were still in the canyon, and didn't look as though they were about to move. The problem was whether to wait to see if they would leave or explore the other way down. He knew he and the boy didn't have enough water to hole up forever, and there was always the chance the mules would be discovered by the Indians or Ramirez, whose precise whereabouts was the unknown factor in the equation. He decided time meant everything, action was best, and influencing events better than letting them take their own course. With action in mind, he shook the boy awake.

'They're still there boy. You're going to have to wait here on your own while I take a look at that other trail.'

Billy eyed him suspiciously. 'Why can't I come with you?'

' 'Cos I think Ramirez could be pretty close and one can move better than two.'

'How do I know you'll come back, that they haven't got you?'

'You won't know, kid. Guess you'll just have to hope.'

Billy bit his lip betraying his anxiety. 'Don't like being anywhere near those 'paches.'

'If they leave,' Gannon told him, 'work your way back to where we left the mules and wait there for me.'

Billy still didn't look too keen as Gannon shared out the water and set off back to the mules. He was pleased to find them still there. Mounting his own mule, Gannon picked his way along the same trail they'd used yesterday, moving with extreme caution now he knew those Apaches were so near. With the heightened tension, his nerves were taut. He could have done with a drink but he guessed it was a good thing he didn't have a bottle or he'd have been tempted to drink it all down, and he knew he couldn't afford to impair his senses, especially that sixth sense that made the difference out here.

After an hour of plodding progress he found the trail he was seeking, but he was too cautious to use it. Instead, he climbed higher, and found a place suitable for studying the lie of the land.

His caution proved providential when he caught the flash of a rifle barrel amongst high rocks overlooking the trail; if he'd ridden straight in he'd be a dead man by now for sure. The knowledge gave him two choices: either ride away and back to Billy, or remove the obstacle. He decided on the second course, even though it would take time to climb that rock and kill whoever it was that was guarding the trail, be it an Apache or a *bandito*.

It took him over an hour, working his way on foot and using all the cover available, to reach the rock and start to climb. Each foot placement became even more important because one stumble, one dislodged rock, would mean he was finished. Then, at last, sweat pouring down him in rivulets, he saw the man's back up ahead and drew back into cover, relieved it was a *bandito* and not an Apache. It made him afraid too, because it meant that Ramirez couldn't be far away.

He felt for the knife in his belt, withdrew it and held it by the hilt; this killing would have to be done in cold blood because he couldn't risk a shot. For extra stealth he removed his boots, then stepped out into view, hoping his quarry wouldn't take it into his head to turn at the crucial moment. He started forward, knife held high, ready to plunge it into the Mexican's back as soon as he was within striking distance.

His attention was riveted on the man's spine. As the distance decreased, he was aware of his own breathing, each intake and exhalation exaggerated. It seemed to him it must surely reach the ears of his victim, warning him. But he made it to within a few feet, raised the knife and prepared to deliver the killing blow.

At the critical moment, something the boy said at the spring about killing a man in the back nagged at him. He hesitated, the knife poised mid-air. In that fraction of second the Mexican, warned by instinct, sensed something amiss. He turned, eyes widening when he saw the gringo with the weapon raised to deliver his death warrant. One hand scrambled for the rifle which lay at his side but Gannon, suddenly active again, kicked it away and brought the knife down into his chest, falling on top of the man with the impetus of the strike.

The blade twisted and the Mexican moaned. Gannon was close enough to smell the mescal on his breath, to see pain and fear suffuse in the man's brown eyes as his own locked into them. There was understanding too, that death was coming for him. Yet, in his final moment, there was only hatred for the gringo who had stolen his life.

'My *compadres* will kill you,' he gasped 'Take a look gringo . . . they are all around.'

Gannon waited until the light went out of the Mexican's eyes. As the dead man's head lolled to one side, he removed the knife and wiped blood from the blade. Only then did he consider the purport of those last words. What had the man meant when he said his friends were all around? Were others guarding the trail? He figured there was one way to find out. Fearing the worst he stripped the body of its waistcoat and bandoleers, and dressed himself in them. As a final touch he placed the Mexican's black sombrero on his head, picked up his rifle and stepped out into the open.

He spotted one of them a hundred yards away in ambush mode. He'd evidently seen Gannon emerge because he stood up and stared in his direction, his body language betraying uncertainty. Gannon said a silent prayer, raised the rifle above his head waved. The Mexican, falling for the deception, responded with a similar gesture. Then, apparently satisfied nothing was amiss, he resumed his prone position.

Gannon retreated, angry now that he'd wasted so much time and effort, and had put his life at risk for nothing. Sure, he could kill the man he'd just seen, but how many others were scattered down the trail? It would be too risky. Obviously Ramirez had hedged his bets, leaving this trail guarded while he searched.

There was nothing to do but return to Billy and hope the Apaches had taken it into their heads to move on. Trouble was, Ramirez must be pretty close by now, the delays having cost so much time. Try as he might to be optimisic about their chances, Gannon figured they were decreasing rapidly and a choice between Ramirez and Chato's bunch was really no choice at all.

As he returned the same way he'd come, watching all the time for signs the bandits had cut their trail, he endeavoured to think of a way out of the net closing inexorably in on him and the boy. One possibility he considered was to bring the Apaches to Ramirez somehow, or maybe the other way round. They'd be so preoccupied with each other, it would give Billy and him a chance to slip away. He chewed that over until a possible plan formed in his mind. Later, he found sign that the *banditos* were closing in on the area where Billy and he had hidden, and the idea grew ever more attractive as a way to overcome the growing odds against them.

The boy was not with his mule but in the place Gannon had left him. It was evident he was glad to see Gannon return, but not so pleased to hear what he had to report, bearing in mind the Chiricahua had shown no signs of moving on. He understood their position was dire, capture being inevitable if they did nothing.

'There's one thing left to try,' Gannon told him, after he'd outlined the situation, 'but you'll have to trust me no matter how things look.'

'What do you mean?'

Gannon, wondering how the youngster would take it, scrutinized Billy's face.

'You'll have to go down there with me, amongst those 'paches. I got a hand to play and it might work because some of them know me.'

Billy looked dubious. 'I don't think . . .'

'Thinking won't do you no good kid. There ain't time for it. Like I said, you'll have to trust me. Blind faith, they call it. You just gotta believe.'

Billy still looked dubious, 'Can't we go back? Take our chances on that other trail?'

'Back to Ramirez's men? A rock ain't that much different to a hard place, is it?'

The boy was struggling, like someone teetering on the edge of a precipice, delaying the moment he'll have to jump in the water, knowing deep down he'll have to in the end because there's no other way.

'OK,' he said finally, in a small voice. 'I'll have to trust you, won't I?'

'Well, then, whatever happens, even if you don't like it, keep believing. Now, let's go get the mules and start in.'

'Those Apaches scare me,' Billy said, as they set off walking. His face was as white as sand.

'They scare everyone,' Gannon told him, 'but it ain't likely they'll kill you after I say my piece.'

As they started the mules into the canyon and towards the camp, Gannon's words didn't seem much comfort; he was still afraid and unsure. When Apaches appeared as though from nowhere and converged on the riders, Gannon raised his hands, and told Billy to do the same. An Apache grabbed their mules and started to lead them, the others falling in behind, walking in procession towards the lone figure waiting for them. Closer, they both recognized it was Chato, rifle crooked in his arms, surveying them impassively. Just off to the side of the trail were the horribly disfigured bodies of the men they'd watched die yesterday, a grim reminder – if they needed any – of what his people were capable of.

'What you do here, Gannon?' the chief said, his eyes moving over them as though he were a merchant assesssing the worth of goods. 'Like Chato, you are a long way from nowhere, huh!'

Gannon was not fooled by the chief's neutral tone. He knew he would kill both of them on a whim if he said a wrong word. He inclined his head in Billy's direction.

'I have been looking for Chato. I have come to return one of his possesssions.'

The chief's gaze flitted to Billy, then back to Gannon. 'Gannon brings a white boy, one of his own people, back to the Apache. This is a new thing. Why would Gannon do this?'

Gannon glanced at Billy who was clearly bewildered at this revelation. He hoped the boy would remember what he'd told him, trust what he was doing was for the best, not react and spoil things.

'I valued my trade with the Chiricahua. I hope we will do more business. I wish to prove to Chato that he can trust me.'

A low grumbling, pregnant with resentment, arose from the other Apaches. The memory of their friends who'd been killed for their scalps was still rankling. They were wondering if this man had played a part. Even if he hadn't, who was this whiteman to speak of trust? Chato heard their discontent, and aborted their mutterings with a wave of his hand.

'They are wondering how Gannon has the boy. Chato is wondering too.'

Gannon sighed. 'There was an ambush.'

'This I already know,' Chato said impatiently.

Gannon drew a visible breath and continued. '*Banditos* killed some of your people for their scalps. Only this boy survived. That ambush was nothing to do with me. I stole the boy from the *banditos* and when I heard his story brought him back to you. Chato already knows of the ambush but perhaps will not know who was responsible, who scalped his men.'

The chief's gaze turned on Billy, who was listening with an air of mystification, wondering once again whether he could trust Gannon. Was he just trying to save himself, and using him to do it? That was certainly the way it could be interpreted. He had never been entirely sure of the man.

'Is this the truth?' Chato addressed Billy, his voice cold and demanding, anger just below the surface. Billy tried to find his voice but it was too deep in his chest, suppressed by fear. He just nodded affirmation, hoping his trepidation wasn't as salient on the outside as it felt on the inside.

'These *banditos*.' Chato said, turning back to Gannon, eyes narrowing so that they were mere slits beneath their hoods. 'Where are they now?'

'My second gift to Chato. The *banditos* are very close. You can almost reach out and touch them. They are coming for the boy.'

The hoods lifted perceptibly. 'Where?'

'A little way south. Your sentries will see them soon.'

Chato signalled to two of his men. Immediately, they cut two horses from the makeshift *remuda*, mounted up and rode out.

'What does Gannon want in return?' the chief asked. He was smiling inscrutably now mouth open, showing black teeth like jagged mountain peaks. 'Or is it just his love for the Apache that brings him here?'

Gannon saw in Chato's smile that he was not fooled. He tried to keep his composure. This was what he had been leading to, the critical moment. Chato was sagacious: he knew there was something he wanted, that his efforts were not just to maintain a trading advantage. But he might still go along with him.

'The boy is worth money,' he said, not daring to look at Billy. 'His father owns stores in Tucson. He will pay for his son's return.'

'Rifles?' Chato rapped out the word, a gleam in his eye.

'Possibly rifles, but money at least.'

'Ten rifles,' the chief said. 'For ten rifles, ten sacks of flour and blankets for my men I will give him back.'

Gannon was about to argue about the rifles, but the

hard set of Chato's jaw dissuaded him. To an Apache on the run, rifles were a vital commodity. The chief was known for his stubbornness and this was not a good time to test it. In any case, it was a good deal, far better than he'd expected. The boy's father would probably give more.

'This will be possible,' Gannon said. 'Chato is fair.'

'What will Gannon gain from this?' Chato asked with a suspicious sneer.

'The boy's father will be generous to the man who returns his son.'

Chato nodded his large head, and seemed to accept that. 'In two suns a wagon will leave Tucson with the things I ask. We will send smoke and the wagon will follow the smoke.'

'I will arrange it.' Gannon answered, 'when I return to Tucson.'

Chato fixed him with his eyes but the connection was broken as the two riders Chato had sent out returned to the camp. One of them dismounted, approached his leader, and said something in Apache. Chato's reaction was to turn back to Gannon smiling his satisfaction.

'Your words were true. The Mexicans are very close. The sentries have seen them.'

'They know the boy has value and want him back. But they will not know Chato is here.'

Chato's gaze travelled from the boy to the man. 'Be warned, if the wagon does not come we will leave the mountains with the yellow hair in two days.'

'The wagon will come,' Gannon stated emphatically. He paused for a moment. 'May I speak to the boy alone? There are things I need to know about his father before I trade.'

Chato signalled to his men to disperse. 'Speak to him, then be gone. The *banditos* are in my mind now. We will take them soon and you will not like what we do to scalphunters.'

Gannon didn't need convincing. What his men had done to the innocent ranchers and the child after that last trading escapade was burned into his mind. His own shame remained with him, and it always would. Dwelling on that matter could do no good right now. Pushing the memory away, he edged Billy's mule to the side of the trail and spoke quietly to him.

'Like I said, Billy, there wasn't much choice and you're still better off than you were. Two days is all and you'll be home and dry. I wish you luck, meanwhile.'

'You're coming back for me aren't you?' Billy's voice rose a decibel. He was still chalk-white and obviously remembering his previous experiences.

Gannon frowned. 'No need for me to come back. Your pa will come with that wagon and if your pa don't fancy it, he'll hire someone.'

Billy shivered as he glanced over to the Apaches who were daubing their faces with yellow paint, readying themselves for a fight.

'You really trust him?'

'In this, I guess I do.'

Billy cast his eyes downward. 'How can you? You saw what they did.'

Gannon understood the boy's fear well enough, and tried to reassure him.

'Chato depends on trading, for guns in the main, sometimes food. At times, he exchanges hostages for them. He won't want word to get around he can't be trusted in those matters. He can't afford to, the way he lives. That's why he'll let you go.'

Billy looked dubious. 'My pa won't like giving them rifles, will he?'

'He'll keep that quiet. I'll tell him to. Nobody need know. You just keep your chin up and you'll be high and dry soon enough.'

With that, he walked away and mounted his mule. As he rode down the canyon to freedom, Gannon couldn't but help admire the way Billy had taken it. Some youngsters his age would be crying tears fit to fill the canyon, but the kid had kept about as cool as was possible given the situation; he knew men who would have made more fuss. For sure, he felt bad about leaving him like that, but it had seemed the only way – and he'd told him the truth about Chato's need to preserve good faith. Everything was going to be just dandy; he was sure of it. All that remained was to seek out Billy's father and set up the trade. Then his part would be done and he could ride on with an easy conscience, and forget this latest piece of bad luck.

10

The years fell away as Gannon rode along the dusty street into Tucson. The town wasn't much but it held good memories for him, maybe too many. Perhaps that's why he'd never returned in the intervening years. Once you were on a bad road, it was hard to look over your shoulder and remember what might have been. If you did, the present might become unbearable, the future a desert without any succour.

After he'd shot the little girl he'd wandered aimlessly, hit the bottle, and ended up in that Mexican village with nothing. Chance, in the form of the priest and the boy, had at least got him going again. Now, he didn't intend to stop long before heading off to a new life further west.

Trueman's store wasn't hard to find. He hitched the mule and went inside, shaking the dust from his clothes as he stepped across the threshold. His appearance drew curious glances from the customers, but he ignored them and waited patiently until the last one was served before he approached the counter.

The man serving was tall, bearded, much of an age as Gannon. He was leaning forward on his elbows, and though his brown eyes were lively and friendly enough as they assessed the stranger in his store, there was a sadness detectable too.

'Can I help?' the man said.

'I need to talk to the owner. It's a matter of urgency.'

'You're looking at him, mister.'

Gannon glanced around the store, making sure it was empty. 'I need to talk to you in private, Mr Trueman.'

The storekeeper frowned, and studied him warily. Gannon was conscious of how he must look coming straight in off the trail – dirty, dishevelled and mysterious – and didn't blame him for his caution.

'Nobody will come in here. If they do, you can wait till they've gone,' Trueman said pleasantly enough but still circumspect, not willing to trust a stranger too readily.

Gannon sighed. 'It's about your son and it's best said real private.'

'About Billy? What do you know about him? Have you got him? Where is he?' Trueman became animated, firing the questions in rapid succesion, his anxiety plain. Gannon knew, from the distasteful way he was looking at him, he suspected him of involvement in Billy's kidnap or something worse.

'He's safe but getting him back ain't going to be straightforward.' Gannon nodded to a door at the back. 'Can we go through there?'

Trueman lost his previous inhibition and started

round the counter. Gannon noticed he moved awkwardly, leaning heavily on the counter for support. When he emerged he saw the reason: the man only had one leg; the other was just a stump. Using a chair for support, Trueman bent over and picked up a crutch which was lying on the floor. Then he started for the door with surprising agility, beckoning for Gannon to follow.

The back room had the semblance of an office. There was a table with two chairs and they sat facing each other, the shopkeeper's eyes never leaving Gannon for a moment. There was an anticipatory gleam in his eyes too, and he was plainly impatient for news of his son as he studied the stranger.

'Now, tell me about Billy,' he said. 'Where is he? Is he safe?'

'I left your son with Chato and his Chiricahuas but he's well and he's going to be safe. That is he'll be safe if you go along with the chiefs demands.'

Trueman's face turned ashen. In contrast the bags under his eyes, the legacy of too many worrying nights no doubt, were exaggerated to black half-circles. He shot Gannon a disgusted look.

'You're working with the Apaches, mister. . . . A go-between, huh?' Trueman shook his head disbelievingly. 'I'd heard there were men like you but I didn't believe it. Working against your own kind is pretty low.'

'The name's Gannon, Jim Gannon, and you got me all wrong. I ain't working with Chato or anyone. Just hear me out and you'll understand.'

He went on to explain the events from the moment

he'd first laid eyes on the kid. He stressed that leaving Billy with Chato had been calculated, the only way out, and though Chato had slaughtered the men sent to look for Billy, he thought the Apache was sure to trade fair, and gave reasons why he thought so. Trueman listened with rapt attention until he'd finished. A little shamefaced, he apologized.

'I'm sorry, guess you ain't working with them. I've been under strain since Billy disappeared and assumed the worst about you.'

'Understandable in the circumstances, and I ain't lily-white for sure,' Gannon said with good grace. 'So you'll arrange for Chato to get what he wants and get your son back?'

'Of course. No choice, have I?' the storekeeper agreed, but he was frowning as he continued. 'I don't like giving them guns though. The folks here won't like it either, especially after that search party was butchered.'

'Now you see why I wanted this conversation private. Best you keep what's happening quiet so nobody interferes and messes it up. You'll want everything to go smooth for the boy's sake.'

Trueman stroked his beard and searched Gannon's face with those brown eyes, as though trying to read beneath the surface of the man. His thoughts finally came to the surface.

'Would you take the wagon to Chato? I'll pay you well if you will.' He blushed with embarrassment. 'This leg is a bit of a handicap on a rough ride but I'd go with you.'

Gannon leaned back in his chair and held up his hands, a barrier between them.

'I've had my fill of trouble. I'm heading west soon as I can. Other thing is, only one man can go with the wagon. Chato made that plain as day.'

Trueman's head went down, his disappointment clear. He mumbled, 'I shouldn't have asked. You've been through enough.'

Gannon felt pity for the man but not sufficient to change his mind. 'There are men in this town who'll do it for money and keep quiet. You'll find someone, no trouble.'

'I guess.'

A silence developed. Gannon could see Truernan was preoccupied with thoughts of his son, was already working out how he would deal with the matter of the exchange. He figured his part was over and rose from the chair.

'Got a powerful thirst,' he said.

Trueman used his crutch to haul himself up. He continued to look distracted.

'Forgive me, I was thinking about Billy and forgetting my manners.'

They went back into the emporium where the storekeeper hopped back behind the counter, opened the till, grabbed a handful of notes and pushed them into Gannon's hand.

'Guess you'll need this,' he mumbled. I'm grateful for what you did for the boy. Guess it's up to me now.'

Gannon had no scruples about taking the money. He figured he'd more than earned it.

'Thanks,' he said and added, 'You've got a good boy, Trueman. I hope it all goes well. No reason it shouldn't.'

He believed what he said, at least in the main. His reservation was that, when you were dealing with Apaches, nothing was ever one hundred per cent certain. Trueman would know that; every man in the territory knew it. But, thankfully, that was none of his business now. He liked the boy, respected his fortitude but, as the father had just said, he'd done enough. He wanted a bit of peace, and trouble was something he was trying to put behind him if it would let him, a part of the life he'd been attempting to jettison before this business had enmeshed him through no fault of his own.

'You staying around?' Trueman called after him as he headed for the door.

'Maybe a day or two,' Gannon said over his shoulder.

Outside, he surveyed the street and saw the sign for the saloon still hanging over the low-roofed adobe building across the way. He'd managed to do without a drink while his mind had been occupied out there in the mountains, but he was feeling an increasing need now that the pressure was off. Trueman had provided him with the cash, and he'd still have plenty left over for his other needs if he took a few slugs to relax himself.

He crossed the street, entered the building, and was surprised to see the main room busy since it was still early. His presence initially drew the usual curious glances reserved for any stranger in town, but the clientele returned to its business when he made straight for the bar and settled there without paying anybody any attention.

'Whiskey,' he told the barman. Figuring he had

enough cash to celebrate his return properly, he added, 'A glass and a bottle.'

He poured himself a drink, slugged it down, then poured another which he drank at a slower pace, relishing that familiar burning sensation in his throat. Fragments of conversation from the men along the bar drifted to his ears as he drank. He didn't tune in immediately because part of his mind started speculating about the woman. Was it possible Mary was still in town? The priest had said he should try to seek her, out, ask forgiveness for the way he'd just left her, clear his conscience. But it was all so long ago; it was an act of foolishness to dwell on it. Down there, exiled in that Mexican town and away from everything familiar, his mind hadn't been right. Anyway, it was more than likely she'd be long gone by now. Time moved on. It was all foolishness on his part, a temporary aberration which he'd get over.

His reverie was interrupted by the words he heard from further along the bar. At first, he couldn't believe their purport and thought he was imagining it – either that or his conscience was playing a trick, distorting harmless words into translations he didn't want to hear.

'Just a little girl, no more than three years old.' A bulky man, the speaker, was shaking his head, his tone morose.

'Where was this, Jim?' one of his drinking cronies enquired.

'About ten miles west, near the mountains. First off, she'd been skewered and hung up like she was meat. One of the scum had taken her outside and blown her brains out after that. Surprising they put a bullet in her head. Seemed almost merciful from those savages.'

'You said the Apaches did for all the family.'

'All except one of the brothers. He was here in Tucson. When he heard he just went crazy, never recovered either. It's not a pretty thing seein' a good man go mad.'

Gannon felt himself redden. He could hardly believe what he was hearing. Was there no place he could escape from it and find a bit of peace from his conscience? A vision of the little girl in his arms as he carried her out of the building floated up from his past, and he relived it all again. The merciful bullet exploding in her brain, his only recourse to speed up her dying agony, had ended it for her. Like sharp shards of glass pricking his soul, each detail returned to him now, giving the lie to time's passage. The bottle in front of him loomed like his only saviour.

He wanted to get drunk, to burn the girl out of his head with liquid fire. But he still had enough of his faculties working to comprehend when he felt someone tug at his sleeve. He looked into the old, grizzled face of the man at his elbow.

'Yeah!' he snapped, angry his mind's journey into blissful, whiskey oblivion was a long way from over.

'You the feller just rode in to see Trueman?'

'That's me!' He picked up the bottle and started to top up his glass again, paying scant attention to the newcomer.

'Mrs Trueman asked me to find you. She'd like to speak to you. She's anxious about her son.'

He stopped pouring, 'The mother?'

'Billy's mother, yeah.'

Gannon shrugged. 'Maybe later. Right now I'm doing some serious drinking.'

'Mister, Mrs Trueman's a lady. She shouldn't have to be kept waiting without good reason. To me you don't look like much of a gent. Maybe you shouldn't bother seeing her at all. I'll tell her I couldn't find you.'

Gannon's bad temper resurged. Who was this old timer to bother him, to talk down to him?

'Suits me,' he muttered. 'Just leave me be.'

The old timer seemed to hesitate. Gannon ignored him. Next time he turned, he was gone.

He drank steadily until the bottle was finished, and felt better with each glass. Trouble was, his alcohol tolerance was high; he would have liked another bottle to do the job properly. For once, prudence got the better of him; he gave in to the fact he didn't have so much money that he could squander it, especially when he'd be hitting the trail soon and would need supplies.

When he left the saloon, he was half-drunk. Outside, the fresh air revived him sufficiently to remember the old timer's message. In a vague, muddled way induced by the whiskey, he figured he owed Frank Trueman. He had time on his hands, so he asked someone where the Truemans resided and was directed to the one of the houses at the edge of the town.

11

The house, painted a pristine white, was pretty from the outside. There were colourful flowers in the window and the small garden showed signs of caring cultivation. Gannon mused that Trueman was lucky. There was something about the place. It exuded a feeling of calm, as though you could find a haven here, put your troubles aside, forget what went on in the world. He decided he envied the storekeeper his home, and wished he had built a place like it long ago. Then he laughed at himself; chance would have been a fine thing.

He went through the gate, rapped on the door too loud, and wondered what manner of woman the storekeeper's wife might be. It was obvious why she wanted to see him. She would want to know how her son was faring in captivity. All he would have to do was reassure her Billy would be back in two days and be on his way.

The door opened slowly. He caught a glimpse of a female figure hovering uncertainly behind it and, managing to remember his manners, removed his hat.

There was a rustling of skirts and when the figure stepped out on to the threshold, he kept his head politely inclined.

'I'm the feller who was with your son, ma'am,' he opened, 'I guess . . . .'

His voice faded away as he looked into the woman's face. Recognition hit him a hammer blow so that he visibly reeled. The effect on the woman was no less potent. Her sharp intake of breath reached his ears, synchronized with his own unbalancing.

He managed to regain a measure of composure but, like the woman, seemed unable to find words. All they could do was stare at each other. Feeling embarrassed, he started to fiddle with the brim of his hat while trying to come to terms with the fact that Mary Brannigan, the woman he'd left years ago, was standing right there in front of him and could only be, must be, Billy's mother. Fate had a peculiar sense of humour, he thought to himself when he could finally believe the evidence before his eyes.

'Jim Gannon.' She was shaking her head disbelievingly as she found her voice, but her tone was neutral, edging towards cold. 'I can't believe . . . . You're not the one who found my son.'

The question confirmed she was Trueman's wife all right. He was wishing now that he wasn't halfway to being drunk.

'It was me, Mary.' He gestured with his hat towards the interior. 'Can I come in?'

Continuing to look perplexed, she turned, then beckoned him. He entered, followed her into the living-room, and flopped awkwardly into a large armchair when, with a limp, half-hearted gesture, she offered him a seat.

Glancing around the room, he noticed that the tasteful interior matched the initial appearance of the building; this was a real, lived in home, not one of those cold mausoleums just for show. Again he envied Trueman, reflecting that maybe, if he'd had the sense to settle with Mary, he could have had a home something like this.

She seated herself across from him, and made a visible effort to compose herself. For the first time he realized that though the strain of her son's disappearance was etched into her features and her eyes were puffy from crying, the years had been kind to her. The yellow hair, so much like his own and Billy's too, wasn't showing much sign of grey and she didn't look any heavier in the figure. All in all, she'd worn a lot better than he had; he figured that must be down to the good life Trueman was providing.

He was conscious she was inspecting him now the way he had her and flushed, realizing he was unkempt, dressed like a saddle tramp and that she must have detected he'd shifted some booze before this visit. She'd probably smelt it on his breath and, like as not, that old timer had informed her about his boorish behaviour in the saloon.

'Tell me,' she said, her voice hardly warm, as though there was no past between them, as though they'd never known each other at all, 'are you sure Billy is all right, that we'll get him back.'

Gannon's eyes drifted round the room, not meeting hers. 'He's healthy and unharmed and I reckon Chato is sure to trade. You'll have him back in a couple of days.' He added, 'He's a good boy, a credit.'

'You know my husband intends to go out there alone. He tells me you won't go.' Her voice, colder now than he could ever remember from the old days, disconcerted him. Yet what else could he have expected or deserved?

He met her gaze briefly; he couldn't hold it, and lowered his own. 'I'm moving on. Had enough of these parts. Going to California Someone will go in your husband's place. I've seen too much. . . .'

He was aware how lame that all sounded. The way Mary was looking at him, he knew that was exactly what she was thinking. To her, he must seem like a broken man. His pride didn't like that.

'He won't trust anyone to keep silent about the rifles,' she said. 'So he'll go himself even though that leg of his is a handicap. If things did go wrong he couldn't do much.'

'Change his mind for him,' Gannon said.

She shook her head. 'He's stubborn and he's got a point. About the rifles I mean. The townsfolk are touchy about the Apache and anyone giving them weapons will be lynched.' She suddenly wrung her hands. 'Especially after what they did to that little girl. You must have heard.'

Gannon started to sweat. There it was again, the second time that day, rising like a phoenix, returning to haunt him for his wrongdoing. The sooner he left the territory and the incident well behind him the better. He couldn't look at Mary. Why was he here anyway? The room suddenly became oppressive and he knew he had to get out of there. He sprang from the chair as though he'd been sitting on hot coals, and started to edge for the door.

'Got to be going,' he muttered into his chest. 'Don't worry about Billy.'

He was out of the living-room door before she had a chance to respond. All he could think of was getting as far away as possible. But she was following him to the front door and he knew he'd have to turn and face her. Like a child with a guilty secret, he spun round and mumbled what had been on his mind.

'Mary, all these years I've felt bad about leaving, guilty going off just like that. I'm really sorry. Want you to know that.'

Her face reddened and he saw her coldness had suddenly given way to anger as she appraised him. When she spoke, it was with scorn.

'You did me a favour Jim, in the end. After you left, I met my husband and he's been a better man for me than you ever were, and ever could be.' She paused, her bitterness reaching for crescendo. 'No need to feel guilty. Not guilty about that, not about me.'

He was dumbfounded. The priest had told him an apology, making his peace with Mary would help him escape his demons. Instead, she was blazing mad at him and he was feeling worse. And she wasn't finished with him yet.

'You're still running away aren't you, Jim? Always the

easy way with you.' She injected more scorn. 'Always a quitter.'

'What do you mean, Mary? I'm truly—'

'Don't even know what I'm talking about do you, Jim?'

'What. . . ?' His eyes were heavy now, the booze taking its toll, his brain reeling from her onslaught.

'You could go back for my boy,' she said. 'You left him there. You got out of it and now you want to run away. You haven't changed one bit Jim Gannon. Apologizing to me for something that happened years ago and my Billy in the hands of those savages where you put him. Saved your own skin didn't you, Jim?'

'Mary . . . I—'

'Get out!' she screamed at him. 'Just get out!'

She was hysterical. He raised a hand gently to her shoulder but she knocked it aside, and ran away into the bowels of the house, weeping.

Gannon turned back to the door. A sense of loss, regret and guilt intermingling with the effect of the whiskey, he stumbled outside and made his way down the path. Why, he wondered, had the priest imagined he could find peace here? It had not been like that at all, just the opposite. He had reopened old wounds was all. Far from feeling better for it, he felt lousy, and was struggling to think straight. Mary had flown at him, accused him of cowardice, of leaving the boy to save himself. He'd done it to save both their lives, hadn't he? How could she blame him for that? Ironically, in the old days, all she had ever wanted was for him to walk away from trouble. For certain, there were better men than him for the job of rescuing Billy; it was up to her husband to arrange it. The quicker he was out of there and heading west the better. To hell with her and everything else.

Gannon slept off the booze in a stable, out like a light all night but waking next morning with a hangover. After delicately dusting himself down, he stepped through the door into the glare of the sun which did nothing for his aching head. To revive himself, he dipped his head in the water trough.

Yesterday's events were nagging at him. Mary's scathing words were echoing in his head worse than the hangover. He figured what he needed was a good breakfast; it was a while since anything substantial had passed his lips and he was ready for food now.

Just down the street, the sign for 'Martha's Place' caught his eye. He remembered eating there in the old days, sometimes with Mary. Martha, who had been close to Mary, would be getting on now, he supposed, and might not even remember him. He recalled her as a kind, motherly figure who made huge breakfasts. The thought drove him down the street with his mouth watering. A good meal would set him up before he hit the trail.

He entered the premises and found a table by the window. It was still early and he was pleased the few customers occupying the neatly-laid tables weren't taking much notice of him. He didn't want any more confrontations or surprises.

A young girl took his order and brought him a huge plateful of bacon, beans and sausages, which he washed down with copious amounts of coffee. As he ate, he even felt civilized, and promised himself soon he'd start to live like this – sitting at a table with a cloth, using a knife and fork. Age should bring a certain dignity into life and for a long time it had been lacking in his.

'Jim Gannon!'

The voice was familiar even after the passage of years. He'd been so engrossed in the breakfast, he hadn't given his acquaintanceship with the proprietor much thought but he recognized the voice as Martha's. When she came to his table and stood over him, he saw that her hair, greying when he'd left, was pure white and that there were a few more lines on her face. But her eyes were what he remembered most, and it was the warmth and mirth in them that belied her age, making her the same old Martha.

He started to rise but she motioned for him to sit again, and stood over him with her hands on her hips. Her ample figure, swollen by a voluminous pinafore, added to the impression of a solicitous mother hen, watching protectively over her brood but not prepared to stand any nonsense or evasions.

'Hullo, Martha!' He rubbed a hand over his stomach, gestured at his plate. 'My stomach remembers and hasn't been disappointed.'

Her eyes narrowed as she looked him up and down and a worried look passed across her face. Whatever it was bothering her, it doused the warmth and mirth in those eyes, as though she was seeing a black cloud lingering somewhere in an otherwise blue sky, spoiling what might have been a good day.

'I don't look that bad, do I Martha? Nothing one of these here breakfasts won't fix?'

The merriment flashed back into her eyes. 'Nothing a good bath and a set of new clothes wouldn't fix, you mean. What happened to you, Jim? Just look at you.'

'Not much, Martha,' he answered, smiling. 'Not much of note, anyhow.'

Her face grew serious. 'I spoke to Mary after you left her yesterday. She told me you were with Billy and left him with the Apaches. That was hard for me to believe.'

He played with the fork. Not looking at her, he mumbled. 'It was the only way open, all I could do at the time for both our sakes. Chato will trade the boy. She tell you that?'

'She told me. She also told me that her husband is going alone, that you've washed your hands of it.' Martha hesitated. 'She married a good man, Jim, but he ain't up to it, not with that leg of his.'

'A better man than me were her exact words,' he said, moodily. 'She really rubbed that in. Left me in no doubt.'

Martha sighed impatiently. 'She's concerned about Billy, you fool. Sometimes women say things in frustration. Anyway, you deserved all you got from her, Jim. She waited for you and you never came back, never even wrote.'

He nodded his head, slowly and affirmatively. 'You got that right, Martha. I was foolish. I wanted to tell her how sorry I was for a long time but when I did, it didn't help.'

She eyed him shrewdly. 'You missed the obvious way

to make it up to her didn't you?'

'How's that?'

He was wishing now he'd never come here. He just wanted to forget about it, ride on, but it seemed Martha wanted to press a point. She was looking to the heavens as though praying for patience.

'Go fetch Billy back for her, you idiot. Surely it don't need spelling out.'

'I've had enough,' he mumbled with a shrug of his shoulders. 'I vowed to keep out of trouble. Sometimes you're full up, Martha . . . saturation point . . . then all you want is peace or you'll go over the edge.'

His voice had risen with emotion. The other diners were staring at him. Surprised at himself, he was embarrassed, a little ashamed. He reached for the coffee cup, drained it in one go and made to rise.

'Sit right back down and listen, Jim Gannon,' Martha commanded, her tone brooking no argument. 'There's things you have to hear and since Mary won't tell you, I guess it's up to me to stick my big nose into other folks' affairs just like I've been doing all my life.'

With an air of resignation, he leaned back, folded his arms and prepared himself for another character assassination.

'Mary might have called you a coward but she doesn't really believe that and neither do I. Something happened to you, Jim Gannon. What exactly, I don't know, nor care to.'

'It surely did,' he muttered resentfully, thinking of the little girl.

Martha drew in her breath. 'When Billy was a little

kid he got in the way of a team of spooked horses that took off down front street. Frank saw the wagon headed for Billy and ran out, and managed to push him out of the way just in time. Trouble was his own leg went under the wheel.'

'A brave man,' Gannon said, meaning it. 'Billy has that in him too. Like his father, I guess.'

Martha waited until Gannon, who was wondering why she had gone quiet, looked her right in the face. Then her words plunged into the silence, like a sudden rush of water as it accelerates to meet the waterfall's edge where nothing can stop it.

'He's not Frank's son, Jim. He's yours. Billy is your son.'

Gannon couldn't take the words in. His son? Billy? His jaw dropped. He tried to conjure Billy's face. There was a certain likeness, he supposed. The blond hair . . . but Mary's hair was blonde too. She would have told him, surely. But how could she have? He'd left her behind, gone wild.

As though from a distance, he heard Martha say. 'Frank knows he's not his son. Doesn't know who the father is. He treats Billy like a son though. Always has.'

His mind was reeling. It had hit him hard; he didn't know what to think or feel. Then shock gave way to resentful anger. He felt as though part of himself had been excised without his knowing. Like pain in a phantom limb, he could feel it now. He could have lived another life if he'd known, a better life. Mary could have tried to find him. Why hadn't she tried? Finally, guilt at his own behaviour surfaced. Why had he treated the kid, his son, so brusquely up there in the Sierras?

Martha kept quiet, giving him time to absorb it. When he eventually looked at her, he could see she was wondering if she'd done the right thing, telling him this after so much time had passed.

'Mary found she was pregnant just after you left that last time,' she said.

'I guess,' he answered in a reedy whisper.

'She won't like me telling you. But I figured there comes a time and this is it.'

He leaned forward, folded his arms on the table. 'You say he's a good husband, a good father to my son?'

'The best on both accounts. Never let that leg of his get in the way. Built up a thriving business and the folks round here respect him.'

Gannon stood up, took some bills from his shirt pocket, and placed them on the table. He touched Martha's shoulder lightly.

'You did right Martha, telling me. A man should know a thing like that. She should have told me somehow.'

'What will you do?' she called out as he pulled on his hat and headed for the door.

There was hurt and confusion in his eyes as, with his head hung low, he looked back at her from under the brim.

'Don't know,' he said, huskily.

'Then you should,' she stated. 'You should know.'

As he was closing the door, he heard her shout. 'It'll come to you, son, or I've wasted my time telling it.'

His emotions were a maelstrom as he stood in the

street, looking first one way then another, unable to think straight, unable to decide even in which direction he should go. He had a son! That was really something, but the revelation had been like receiving a most precious present only to have it snatched back the next moment, because the reality was that Billy had been brought up by another man. Too many wasted years had elapsed for it ever to be different, for him to make it different. In his confusion, his gaze wandered in the direction of the Trueman home. Something inside that needed release, or it would eat at him forever, propelled his legs in that direction.

He went up the path like an automaton, rapped on the door and waited, his hurt and confusion imploding. Mary opened the door, saw the angry look in his eyes, and made to shut it. His foot shot out and prevented her. With all his strength, he pushed the door wide open.

Mary stared, wide-eyed. Wringing her hands, she screamed. 'Why can't you just leave me in peace.'

'You didn't tell me,' he shouted. 'All those years! You didn't tell me.'

She drew further back and seemed to shrink. She realized he knew now but it didn't alter the hateful way she looked at him.

'My son wasn't going to be a bribe to bring you back,' she yelled. 'You wanted to be free and I let you.'

'Your son! Your son! He was my son too!'

Her tone was scornful. 'Face it, Jim. You were a waster. You had too many chances. What kind of father would you have made?'

'You never gave me a chance, not with the boy,' he yelled.

She gripped the door with both hands. 'You just had a chance and what did you do? You left your son with those murdering savages. That's what you did with your chance.'

Gathering all her strength, she slammed the door in his face. He stood there staring at the wooden panel, the complicated knots in the line of the grain almost up against his eyes. His own thoughts were just as abstruse; he resented Mary for excluding him from his son's life but something was whispering insistently there was some justification in that.

He walked back to the stable miserable, and decided what he had always intended was best. He'd get out of Tucson, leave all this behind him, start a new life. There was nothing for him here. His life, his place, had been usurped. The woman he'd loved was another man's wife, the son he hadn't known about belonged to the same man. Life was playing a joke on him just when he was trying to staighten out.

Within the hour he'd packed and paid the stable owner. Riding out, he passed Martha's place, aware of the old woman watching him go from behind her curtains. But, in the mood he was in, he never looked in her direction or raised his hand in farewell.

12

As he rode westward, he tried to banish his self-pity. Dwelling on things too much might lead him down a dark road he'd already been travelling for too long. But his thoughts kept returning to places he didn't want them to go, kept nagging at him to stop and think, to do the right thing.

At noon, he stopped to let the animal drink at a waterhole, then took some refreshment himself. It was while he was resting near the water that his anger at Mary, at life, but mostly at himself, diffused a little so that he was able to think straight.

The truth crept up on him gradually and it was hard to face. Mary had been right about him. He hadn't had it in him to settle down in the old days. A son would have made a difference, of course, but he couldn't swear even now it would have made enough of a difference. How could he have expected Mary to believe it would when he wasn't sure himself? Anger at things he couldn't change had made him fire off at her and he felt ashamed.

Then, he did what he'd tried assiduously to avoid all morning: he thought about the boy, his son, and his shame mushroomed. In that Mexican town he'd rejected Billy's plea for help; it had taken him so much time to give him water he'd asked for. When the priest had set off to rescue the boy, he'd kept his role safe and minimal, and had thought of himself first. He put his head in his hands; the priest had given his life for his son when it should have been him.

Gannon wiped the sweat that poured from his brow, but he couldn't wipe away the memories assailing him from all sides. The boy had been brave throughout his ordeal while he had been thinking mainly how he could extricate himself from the situation. He saw the hard truth was that he was so used to living with himself, he'd had no room for kindness. The death of the little girl should have taught him something. Whatever strange law operated the universe was punishing him, showing him the consequences of his actions, making him see that he'd moulded himself into a man able to turn his back on his own flesh and blood. Tears ran down his face, mingling with his sweat.

He sat there a long time. In California there would be a new start, but would he ever escape the memory of the past? He'd been trying to forget, using booze as a crutch. The priest had tried to help him. When he'd told him about Mary, his advice had been to seek forgiveness. That way the slate would be clean, the priest had said. Then it came to Gannon, with blinding clarity, that he had been given a chance to make something up to his son and to Mary now.

Knowing what he had to do, he mounted up and glanced westwards at the horizon. Shaking his head, denying the temptation, he spun the animal round and set off back to Tucson.

Gannon tied his horse at the hitching rail opposite the store and watched from a narrow alleyway. He was relieved to see Trueman had not left for the hills, and was at that moment supervizing loading the wagon. It looked like he'd made it back just in time but he couldn't move in, not until the youths who were loading for the shopkeeper had disappeared; he needed to speak to Trueman alone, and better here than out on the trail.

The last item to be lifted on to the wagon surprised him. He could make out the word dynamite on the box one of the youths placed under the seat and guessed Trueman, all power to him, had decided to take a little insurance policy along with him in case the trade with Chato went wrong.

When he'd paid the youths, the shopkeeper hopped up the steps on his crutch and re-entered the store. It was what Gannon had been waiting for. He hurried across the street, entered close behind him, and stood silently inside the doorway.

Trueman, busying himself loading a rifle, did not see him at first. When he realized someone was there, he squinted in his direction, and showed surprise when he recognized him. Gannon noticed his face was gaunt and drawn. For a moment he just studied the shopkeeper silently, then he closed the door behind him, barred it and stepped further into the room.

Trueman's mouth dropped open. 'What do you think you're doing, mister?'

'Want a quiet word. Don't want anyone overhearing,' Gannon answered. He walked across the floor to stand close to him.

Trueman's grip on the rifle tightened. 'Thought we'd said everything. I'm mighty glad you came to Tucson with the news about Billy but right now I'm real busy.'

'You decided to go alone?'

'No choice. Ain't going to trust anyone else. He's my son and I don't want this messed up. Shouldn't even have asked you.'

'I'll go.'

Trueman looked stunned. 'That's a swing around ain't it?'

'A man can change his mind, can't he?'

'Why would you change yours?'

'Got to thinking. Because I started it, I should see it through.'

When he spoke again, the scepticism written all over Trueman's face was matched in his voice. 'My wife said she tried to convince you and you wouldn't buy it. She said she knew you once. Her view is I probably couldn't trust you to see it through.'

Gannon drew in his breath and restrained himself

from blurting the truth straight out. But Trueman was going to take more convincing than he'd imagined and he knew there was no other way to persuade him except with the truth.

'Mister, there's things I got to say and I figure you're man enough to hear them.'

Trueman sighed impatiently and rested his rifle on the counter. 'Spit it out quick then,' he said. 'I ain't got time for long speeches today.'

Gannon gave it to him bluntly. 'Billy's my son, which fact I didn't know, until yesterday.'

He watched Trueman's face. The man was taking it well, showing no outward reaction, no matter what he might be feeling inside.

Eventually, the storekeeper said calmly, 'Guess that's not unlikely. Always knew he wasn't mine. But that don't change anything. Mary said you can't be trusted and the boy's as good as my own son. I'm going alone, mister.'

'No, Frank! 'Fraid you ain't!'

Trueman's face flushed. His jaw jutted determinedly and he picked up the rifle in one hand. Leaning on his crutch, he started for the door.

'Try and stop me!'

Gannon knew then he had to act, though he wouldn't like himself for it afterwards. Resigning himself to that, he took a step to the side and kicked out at the crutch. The storekeeper stumbled, fought for his balance, and lost it. As he went down, he tried to swipe Gannon with the rifle barrel. Gannon sidestepped away, caught hold of the weapon and pulled it from his grasp.

Then he kicked the crutch to the far corner of the room.

Trueman hit the floor hard, rolled over on to his back and stared up at Gannon. Hatred, frustration and shame vied in his expression while he cursed the man who'd taken advantage of his handicap. For his part, Gannon felt the keen bite of shame for what he'd done to a good man.

'Frank Trueman,' he said, 'from what I hear you're a better man than I ever was and I wish I hadn't had to do that. But this is my time. You've done well as a father to Billy all these years but you don't need to get killed in my place now. One man, a priest, has already done that.'

He walked to the door, unbarred it, opened it up and let the sun in. One more time he glanced at the supine man.

'I'm sorry for what I just done,' he stated. 'But, believe me, in this you can trust me. When it's over and done with, I'll be gone out of all your lives and Billy will never know who I am.'

Gannon strode outside, climbed on to the wagon, flicked the reins at the horses' backs and started for the outskirts of the town. Passing Martha's place, he saw the proprietor standing at the window. He noticed she was smiling; he guessed that was because she'd got him doing what she'd intended all along by revealing he was Billy's father. Strangely, in spite of the danger ahead, he felt justified; it was a feeling he hadn't known for years.

When the town was well behind him, he stopped the wagon and checked that the cargo in the back was secure. Satisfied on that count, he used one of the blankets to cover the box of dynamite, arranging it so that it was just visible under the seat, and set off again for the hills.

13

Gannon scanned the foothills as he drove the wagon across the flat plain. For sure, their scouts would already be watching him, marking his progress in the vastness of that landscape. He knew, if they so chose, they could reach out and swat him as easily as a fly. In the shimmering heat haze, his eyes continued to seek the smoke that would tell him which direction to take. Of course, they would only light their fire when they were sure nobody was following, and were convinced the white eyes from Tucson intended no tricks. He hoped Trueman would have the sense to work that one out, to let him do this his way, not follow him and ruin things.

Finally, he saw the signal: small clouds of black smoke rising and billowing in the sky, like smudges of black thumbprints on a serene, blue backdrop. He changed his direction instantly, and headed straight that way. The place they'd chosen would, he knew, have to be accessible for the wagon; that was some consolation – it meant they probably wouldn't drag him too far into the wild country.

An hour later, muscles aching a little from the bumpy ride, he entered a canyon with a trail only just suitable for the wagon's passage. That was when the first Apache appeared on a high pinnacle, as motionless as the rocks themselves, except for the slight flapping of his breech-cloth when a faint breeze played with its edges. Further in, a second showed himself, near enough so that Gannon could pick out his facial features: the high cheekbones, aquiline nose, his smirk of satisfaction at the prospect of the rifles the white man was bringing to his people. Gannon knew those two had chosen to show themselves, that others watched unseen. He must be close now.

One by one, as though sprouting from the land itself, they appeared and fell in beside the wagon, stone-faced, walking with him like his funeral cortège. It crossed his mind that his dead body was all that was needed to complete the grim parallel.

The canyon curved. When he'd negotiated the bend, their temporary camp appeared ahead. Other Apaches were waiting there. They gathered round the wagon as he eased it into their midst. All the while, he tried to hide his apprehension because he knew the Apaches abhorred any show of fear. One sign of his would lose him respect.

He glanced off to his left, and inwardly recoiled before he could bear to look again. Ramirez and two of his men were lashed to the giant cacti growing near the cliffs on the far side of the canyon. The Apaches had half-skinned them. Gannon didn't want to begin imagining their pain which, exacerbated by the sharp cactus needles penetrating their bodies as though they were pincushions, and would be the quintessence of agony. The Mexicans were in a living hell, just this side of death, and would be praying for the end to come. But he knew the Apaches had only just begun, that Chato would require a slow, drawn-out recompense for the misery the *banditos* had inflicted on his people. In spite of the fact that retribution was fitting, and brought on themselves, Gannon couldn't help but feel their end shouldn't be such an agonizing affair. In his book justice had to be be swift, no matter what the crime.

He climbed off the wagon and concentrated on what he had to do, his face impassive. Apache faces stared into his own, looming close as though to challenge him, adding to his discomfiture as he waited. When the crowd parted, Chato was striding imperiously towards him, a young boy who could have been his son at his side. The Apache renegade halted in front of Gannon, and studied the white man before his eyes fixed on the wagon.

'You have brought the rifles and blankets, Gannon?'

'Just as I said. Give me the boy and two horses and I'll be gone.'

A twisted smile played on the chief's lips. 'You do not wish to watch the Mexicans die. It was you who gave them to us as a present, was it not?'

'I take no pleasure in such things,' Gannon said. 'All I want is the boy.'

Chato walked past him to the wagon and examined the contents. Gannon held his breath, hoping he wouldn't notice the grey blanket hiding the explosives under the seat. After opening the box containing the rifles and handling each in turn the chief faced him, his expression conveying his satisfaction.

'Guns to fight the bluecoats and blankets to keep us warm. This is a good day.'

'I have kept my word,' Gannon said. 'Will Chato keep his?'

The chief raised his hand. Billy was manhandled through the ranks of the assembled Apaches. Gannon felt a lump rise in his throat at the sight of the boy. He was seeing him differently now that he knew he was his son. It was strange to realize the frail figure was part of him that would, all being well, live on and father his progeny. He noticed that Billy's head was up, facing up to his troubles, not letting them see his fear. That gave him strange stirrings of paternal pride.

When Billy saw him, his reaction was relief mixed with surprise. He'd obviously never expected to see him again and Gannon felt ashamed that perception was so near to the truth of the matter.

Chato pushed Billy forward, and signalled for one of his men to fetch two horses from their temporary *remuda.* Gannon put his arm round the boy's shoulder but neither said anything. When the horses arrived, he helped Billy up and mounted himself. Chato held the bridles and Gannon, hoping there was to be no last-minute change of mind on the chief's part, waited anxiously for him to release them.

'Maybe we trade again, Gannon. Maybe you bring more rifles.'

'Chato has kept his word, so maybe I will catch up with him again.'

Chato grinned, showing his black teeth. 'We will have gold for rifles next time.'

Gannon swung his horse away, pulled the boy's after him. It seemed they were going to make it out of there. He should have felt good; instead he was thinking of the little girl he'd had to shoot. Other children like her could be wiped out with those rifles and the dynamite he'd left behind. Once again, he was part-responsible, however unwillingly.

He noticed Billy had seen the Mexicans, and was averting his gaze. He wished he could have spared him that sight and other travails since he'd been taken. Too young, he was seeing the dark side of life.

When they were clear of the camp Billy said, 'I didn't expect you to come.'

'Wasn't going to,' Gannon told him. 'Your father was. I persuaded him to let me instead.'

'Why did you do that? Is he paying you?'

That hurt Gannon but he figured the boy was justifed. 'I reckoned your father was too brave for his own good,' Gannon said. 'And no, he ain't paying me.'

They were some way along the trail when Gannon gave in to what had been scratching ever more frantically at his conscience.

'Can't do it,' he announced. 'Can't let them have those rifles and that dynamite, can't let those Mexicans die that way.'

'There's nothing you can do,' the boy said. 'There's too many of them.'

'Think your pa had something in mind. You just wait for me here Billy. When you hear hell break loose, give me a few minutes. If I don't come just keep heading out of the canyon, then northwards fast. You should make Tucson OK.'

Billy studied him, a little bemused. 'You're different,' he proclaimed. 'I thought you didn't care much about anything.'

Gannon looked into the blue eyes so much like his own.

'Sometimes you look in a mirror and you don't like what you see. One day you'll understand about me and you'll know I tried, even though it was too late.'

With that he spurred his horse back in the direction of Chato's camp. He didn't like leaving his son but he figured that, even if he didn't make it back himself, Billy would have enough time because the renegades would have something else to occupy them for a while.

14

Doubts, like thieves to steal his resolve, crept into Gannon's mind as he approached the camp for the second time. For sure, it wasn't long ago he wouldn't have gone near there in the first place, never mind putting himself in danger without some prospect of advantage to himself.

He wondered if he was just being plain foolish, showing off to the boy. He could still turn round and ride away, of course. But that was an option he knew he couldn't take. The memory of the little girl was a big part of it but he had to admit a burgeoning, genuine desire to do something his son could remember him for in the years to come. It was all he could give Billy now: a glimpse of what he could have been if he hadn't wavered and fallen below the line that marked a good man.

As he'd hoped, the Apaches were still gathered round the wagon in numbers, examining the rifles and blankets like excitable children with gifts. Distracted, they hadn't seen him and he kept riding in, wanting to be as near as possible before his hand was forced. He could see the grey blanket was still under the seat of the wagon, and was grateful that in their enjoyment of the other commodities they hadn't disturbed it.

Finally, one of the renegades spotted him. He shouted to the others, then pointed up the trail, and soon they all turned in his direction, watching his progress. There was no instant fear of the whiteman riding back into their camp, a rifle resting across his saddle horn; their scrutiny was born of curiosity rather than fear of one man alone. Gannon, coiled like a spring inside, hoped they would remain immobile like that a little longer, and give him a chance to do what he had to.

Fifty yards out, he reined in. His horse pawed the ground sending up little swirls of dust as he surveyed the camp. Dryness cracked his throat and constricted his breathing; adrenalin surged through his body without finding an outlet. He was preparing himself for what was coming.

In the *remuda*, a horse, sensing the sudden unnatural silence, snickered its disquiet. Yet, as though mesmerized by his audacity, they made no move towards him, and waited for him to do something. That inertia gave him the time he required; he measured the distance to the tortured Mexicans, and noted the positions of other Apaches apart from those gathered at the wagon.

As their curiosity subsided, he felt the change in atmosphere. An air of expectation hung over the camp. Something was wrong here; the whiteman was taking too long to approach. His whole manner, the way his eyes were asssessing their positions, gave them notice something was amiss, even though he was one man alone and they doubted his power to hurt them.

Judging it to perfection Gannon made his move, lifting his rifle fast and thrusting the stock between his shoulder and cheekbone. With equal speed, he swung the weapon towards the Mexicans, aimed, and fired three shots in rapid succession. Like angry snarls, their echo resounded off the canyon walls.

Like puppets coming to life with one pull on their strings, the Mexicans' bodies jerked violently and then were still again. But those eccentric movements were enough for Gannon to know he had been accurate and it was confirmed when their heads lolled forward on their chests. Their pain was finished and he transferred his aim to the wagon, pumping bullets at the grey blanket under the seat which hid the dynamite.

At last the Apaches started to respond. As though from the mouth of a great, baited beast, a low, angry murmur emanated from them as they started towards the whiteman who had dared to challenge them in their own camp, robbing them of their vengeance against the *banditos.*

That communal rumbling was diminished to an absolute insignificance when the wagon exploded. With a great roar, bits of wood, metal and parts of human bodies flew up to the heavens. Gannon, struggling to calm his horse, watched the results of his action, shocked himself by the power and ferocity of the explosion.

Transfixed, he watched the bits of debris reach their

zenith where they seemed to hang suspended on the air. Then, as though their power had been revoked on a whim, though they were reluctant to yield it, they fell back to earth like heavy rain and littered the area where the wagon had been. Shaken to their core, the remaining Apaches watched this dispersion of the remains of their friends' bodies. It was the last thing they had expected from one man.

Gannon knew he'd struck Chato a blow from which he'd struggle to recover. He saw the remaining Apaches, Chato amongst them, turn their faces away from the débâcle. They were staring at him as though he was an evil god incarnate, sent to reap a harvest of death amongst their tribe. Gone was their famed stoicism; in its place was pure, unadulterated shock and hatred, a white heat voraciously consuming the distance between him and them. He spurred his horse hard, certain the vengeance they would visit upon him – if they could lay their hands on him – would surpass anything they'd extracted from those *banditos* he'd gifted a reprieve.

There was no doubting, once they'd gathered their wits, they would come after him. He just hoped he'd judged it right, that he and the boy would have enough of a start to be able to outrun them, make it back to Tucson with something to spare. If Billy boy was captured again, he'd have himself to blame and that thought made him drive his horse even harder, demanding it gave him its all.

Billy was waiting for him but plainly agitated. Clearly, he'd heard the explosion and was wondering. This was no time for explanations, however, so he slowed but didn't stop. He just hit the rump of Billy's horse and yelled so that it ran after his. Once it was galloping, he adjusted his speed so the two horses ran parallel. When both animals were full out, he heard the boy yelling above the pounding hooves.

'What did you do to them?'

'Blew those rifles to hell,' he yelled, 'and some of those 'paches with them.'

There was no need to elaborate, or discuss consequences. Gannon knew Billy had seen what those Indians could do first-hand, and knew how cruel they could be. It was all the motivation he would need to stay alert as they raced for the canyon exit.

Wary of the Apache lookouts, Gannon constantly glanced at the canyon walls but luck, or the fact the explosion had been a major distraction, worked for them. No shots were fired and they emerged from the canyon unscathed. When they'd been running long enough to be almost out of the foothills, Gannon allowed himself to think it was going to be easy, a straight run back to town.

His optimism turned out to be badly misplaced. Lady Luck had helped carry him this far. Now she stopped smiling and turned her face away when Billy's horse, at the limits of its speed, stumbled. The youngster cried out in surprise as its legs buckled. Though the animal fought to stay upright, the momentum made it an unequal fight. Its balance went entirely so that Billy was hurled through the air to land heavily. Gannon yanked on his reins, leapt out of the saddle and ran to his son's side.

The boy was still conscious and a quick examination revealed no bones were broken. He was just a little stunned, suffering from shock. Gannon knew he didn't have time to nurse him, not with the prospect of Chato on their tail like a wounded bear distraught at the death of its cubs. He realized immediately the fallen horse had broken a leg. Drawing his pistol, he aimed it at the beast's head and put it out of its misery.

The gunshot made Billy jump but brought him right out of his shock. Gannon knelt beside him and helped him sit up. Half his mind was concerned for his son, the other half was concentrating on the back trail, his eyes compelled to drift there. As he carried out his ministrations, his nerves were balancing on a tightfrope, caught between the desire to move fast out of there and the knowledge that going too fast might damage Billy. At any moment, he expected to see Chato appear.

The youngster caught his concern. 'I'll be all right,' he said. 'Don't worry.'

'Got to get moving,' Gannon said. 'Got to ride double now.'

With his help, the boy managed to rise. He took a swig of water from the canteen Gannon offered him.

'I'm sorry,' he mumbled. 'I ain't much of a horseman.'

Gannon mounted up, reached a hand down for him. 'Not your fault, just bad luck.'

As soon as the boy was securely seated, his arms around his father's waist for support Gannon spurred into the horse. He was thinking the odds on them reaching Tucson safely were considerably reduced, still pretty fair but not as good as they were; the delay had cost them and so would riding double. Their chances depended on how quickly Chato had organized himself, how fast those Apache horses could run.

Now that things had turned for the worse, he was wishing he'd never gone back to their camp and put his son at risk. Billy seemed to sense that's what he was thinking.

'You did right to go back,' he shouted. 'You couldn't have left those rifles.'

The fact that Billy understood made Gannon feel a little better, but he knew his feelings would be as inconsequential as their lives if Chato caught up.

'Hold on tighter,' he shouted over his shoulder. 'Can't afford another spill.'

He concentrated all his efforts into guiding the horse safely, running it as fast as he dared with its double burden. It stumbled a couple of times on rough ground but he managed to retrieve the situation without another disaster. If the Apaches weren't in view by the time they were on the flats, he figured they'd have a clean run home and their troubles would be behind them.

When they were out of the foothills, the plain stretching out ahead, he reined in, scanning their back trail. Initially, peering through his own dust cloud, he could see nothing; he thought it was going to be as he'd planned it, that they would make it with room to spare.

He was about to relay the good news to Billy when the remnants of the dust cleared entirely and he glimpsed part of the terrain that it had hidden from him; too near for comfort seven figures were riding full tilt down a sandy declivity, their horses straining against gravity whilst their riders leaned right back in the saddle. They'd made up so much ground, he figured their mounts must be of exceptional quality. Likely, too, their riders had used short cuts that had not been in his own repertoire. Whatever, it was certainly looking grimmer.

Not bothering to explain what he'd seen for fear of frightening Billy, nor wanting to waste a second, he yelled at his horse, spurred harder into its flanks, and demanded it gave him everything now. As soon as they were at full gallop, he focused on nothing but the horizon where he hoped Tucson would appear, a vision of sanctuary to needful pilgrims. But the old maxim was true: time and distance wished away stretch out interminably. That's how it was until, finally, he caught a glimpse of the town which would mean salvation . . . if only.

That first glimpse of the town raised his hopes, but as soon as he glanced over his shoulder to check on their pursuers his spirits descended to the depths. The gods of fortune had only been playing with him, proferring a gift in one hand to snatch it away with the other.

Incredibly, for a people who were not noted horsemen like their Comanche neighbours, the Apaches had closed the gap to two hundred yards, close enough for him to see Chato exhorting his men to greater efforts. One of them was already putting an arrow to his bow as he rode, and Gannon's fear for Billy multiplied tenfold.

He heard the ominous banshee scream of the first arrow as it chased them. The scream transformed to a soft sibilance, like a mother hushing her baby, as it flew past his ear and angled into the ground only yards ahead. He felt Billy's grip on his waist tighten as anticipation of another arrow grasped at his nerve. It was as though he thought Gannon could somehow protect him from the threat behind them if he just held on to him for dear life.

An arrow, closer than the first, so close that Gannon could see coloured twine binding the arrow head to the shaft passed over their heads on a flatter trajectory. He realized, then, it was hopeless to keep running. It would only be a matter of time before one of those arrows found a target and it was more likely to be in Billy's back than his own.

'Got to turn and fight,' he yelled. 'They're too close. Be ready!'

He took the horse round in an arc, hoping the deviation would help to throw the marksmen. When he'd halted the animal, he pushed Billy off, grabbed his rifle and leapt out of the saddle. He hit the ground in a whirl of dust and rolled next to Billy. His free hand reached instantly for the trailing reins whilst the one that held the rifle pushed the youngster flat.

'Take the reins,' he shouted, forcing them into Billy's fist. 'That horse is your lifeline.'

Then, in a blur of movement, he rose to one knee elevated the rifle to his shoulder and fired off two shots in quick succession. His aim was good and like clowns performing circus tricks, two Apaches went backwards off their horses, arms and legs spread exaggeratedly wide. The others, obeying the instinct of their people not to waste lives in needless heroics, reined in and jumped off their mounts. Pulling the animals expertly to the ground, they used them for cover. That done, almost instantaneously one of them fired a shot in Gannon's direction, but the aim was not good and the bullet passed well wide of its mark.

Gannon flattened again. He had to take advantage of the brief respite afforded by his action while the Apaches were considering what their next move would be. His main worry was that they might try to kill the horse which would isolate Billy and him entirely. Turning on to his back, he ejected the spent cartridges from his rifle. As he reloaded, he gave Billy his orders.

'Take the horse and get out of here, Billy. You can see home so keep low and don't stop for nothing.'

When the youngster hesitated, he caught him by the collar, hauled him to his feet, forced his foot into a stirrup, and almost threw him into the saddle. As though to vindicate his actions, another arrow announced itself with a piercing whistle and landed near the horse's back legs.

'What about you. . . ?'

Billy's voice, strained in its appeal, was interrupted by a sharp rebuke. 'Do as I say! Git out of here now! Git!'

Gannon jerked on the reins so the animal was facing Tucson, hit its rump hard and yelled at the top of his voice. Unlike Billy, the horse didn't need a second bidding and burst away, the boy leaning low over its mane.

A bullet biting into the dust between his feet sent Gannon swiftly back to ground. Flat on his belly, he watched Billy galloping away. He was breathing easier, satisfied that his son would survive; the horse was carrying a light load and the Apaches would have to ride over his own dead body to continue the pursuit, either that or make a wide detour which would lose them too much time. Thinking if he didn't survive – which seemed likely – he'd at least got one thing right in his life, he turned his attention to his own defence, determined he wasn't going to give up his life cheaply.

15

When the boy was well clear and the Apaches had made no attempt to circle and pursue the fleeing horse, Gannon knew their main interest was naturally in the whiteman who'd caused them so much grief and damage. The most inimical of them would, of course, be Chato himself. A war leader had to keep his people's confidence, which was not always easy as Apaches were such a susperstitious bunch. Right now, given the disaster Gannon had brought right into their camp, they'd be questioning whether Chato's medicine was strong enough to ward off bad luck.

The plain didn't offer much cover; the ground rose and fell only slightly in places. It was the mesquite growing in scattered patches which bothered him most though. The Apaches would likely use it when they made their move. But right now he felt too exposed, and he considered a patch of mesquite off to his left would offer cover for himself. In a series of crouching runs, he made it without attracting any fire, though he had no doubt they'd have marked his new position.

When he was settled, he did a quick inventory and it didn't improve his opinion of his chances any. There'd been seven Apaches in the pursuit and he'd shot two of them. Of the remaining five, at least one had a rifle. The others would be able to use a bow at that distance, probably to more deadly effect than the rifleman with his weapon. As for himself, he had three bullets left for his rifle and six in his handgun. The one element he considered in his favour was the clock. They'd seen the boy leave and must allow eventually he'd be back with help. That would dictate their tactics because it meant patience, an Apache virtue, would be no use in this scenario; they'd have to come at him fast and furious.

He saw them scattering, leaving their horses, dispersing into the landscape that was their natural milieu, like water seeping into sand until it seems impossible it ever existed at all. Incongruously, a peaceful stillness had descended on the land, as though nothing deadly and sinister was out there. However, the reality was that those human predators would be inching their way forward, vengeance on their minds against the white man who had killed their friends and relatives. That knowledge, his recent exertions, and the heat from an unremitting sun caused his whole body to sweat profusely as his eyes swept the area for a hint of where the attack would begin.

It came when one of them rose like a spectre from the ground. As he propelled himself forward, leaping the scattered mesquite with athletic ease, an unearthly wail issued from his lips. Gannon was startled by the sudden ferocity, even though he'd been expecting this, and took quick aim. In the same instant as the bullet exited the muzzle, the Apache went swiftly to ground. Gannon could only curse at the waste of a precious bullet as the shot passed harmlessly over the point where he'd disappeared.

Hardly had the bullet's whine died away when another Apache, a rifle waving over his head in a mocking gesture, commenced his run forward. His chilling war cry was the equal of his predecessor's. This time, Gannon didn't even manage to get off a shot before he, too, disappeared.

His consolation was that he knew the way they were planning it now. One would run to distract him and, before he could orientate himself, drop out of sight. Another would assume the role, coming at him from a fresh angle. They would alternate their runs like that, pulling the whiteman's attention different ways, confusing him and unsettling his nerve. Gannon was determined he wouldn't succumb and play it their way; he would take the fight to them.

He removed his hat and shirt, and draped them over the mesqite. Next, he scooped up handfuls of dirt and covered his bare torso, rubbing it into his face and neck for good measure. His fair skin suitably camouflaged, he decided a bevel in the ground off to his left would be his first objective. Ignoring the inevitable cuts and bruises he collected on the way, he crawled to it on his belly.

Once there, he settled down to watch, his eyes everywhere. Like an eagle ceaselessly scans its dominion and notices everything, he was attuning himself to the slightest movement. But most of his attention he gave to the spot he'd vacated; he was praying they hadn't spotted his shift to a new position, and if they had, he wouldn't be any better off for his efforts.

Soon the next runner leapt up, took his turn, heading in the direction of the abandoned hat and clothes. It gave Gannon confidence his ruse had worked. Forcing himself to be patient, he ignored their subsequent runs, wanting them so close in he couldn't miss.

When he was sure, he allowed his target three strides before he fired. As though appealing to the gods of the sky at the injustice of his death, the Apache threw his hands in the air and cried out as the bullet penetrated his temple and exited through the top of his skull. He went down, his rifle spinning through the air in front of him.

Gannon didn't allow himself a smidgen of satisfaction before he moved again, on his belly like before. If they'd seen where the shot had come from, he was determined it wouldn't do them any good.

Another Apache rose up and started towards Gannon's hat and shirt, unleashing an arrow as he progressed before discarding his bow and drawing his knife. Full of fury, he leapt at the patch of mesqite which supposedly hid his enemy and scythed downwards with the weapon. He soon discovered his energy was wasted and froze in disbelief. Gannon saw the stupefied look creep into his face, the dawning realization he'd been duped. Then, in his frustration, the warrior thrust the weapon at the material one final time, held it up on the point of his blade so the others would know the reason for his frustration.

The Indian's expression quickly changed from rage to wariness; the whiteman must be lurking somewhere. Gannon chose that moment to pull the trigger. His bullet took the Apache in the chest. The impact drove him backwards but he didn't go down. Instead, he swivelled in Gannon's direction, his free hand dabbing at the blood running from his wound as though he considered it a minor inconvenience, somehow extraneous to him and of little concern. He seemed to sense where the whiteman was hidden and in spite of his wound started that way.

Gannon's ear drums were filled with the pounding of his own heart. His mind was racing faster than the throb of his blood, seeking rationality amidst his tension. He'd used his last rifle bullet. If that Indian kept coming, he would overrun his position and that would force him to break cover. The others would soon take advantage. They'd be on him like a pack of wolves. His alternative was to use the hand gun; it would give his position away but he wouldn't have to stand up as visible as a tree in a desert.

It was the only viable course. Casting the rifle aside, he drew the Peacemaker, and used both hands for a steadier aim. When the buck was almost upon him, so close that he could see the crimson stain on his shirt, the sun's bright twinkle on his knife blade, the wild, disorientated eyes, he pulled the trigger. Like a pig, the Apache exhaled in a loud grunt as another bullet penetrated his chest, shaved the breastbone, and completed its angled ascent to his heart. The gaping cavity spurted a fountain of blood as he tumbled forward, life ebbing out of him even as he fell. His knife was still in his hand as he hit the earth, and it embedded itself in the ground two feet away from Gannon's face.

The future started to unravel too fast for thought. Two of the Apaches, having observed the dead man's stumbling progress towards his position and seen him go down, had decided it was time to risk another rush. Gannon, raising his head, watched as they hurtled towards him from opposite directions. But he couldn't get a good enough shot and didn't want to waste a bullet. Yet, he had to act quickly or they'd be all over him like a rash.

Holding his breath, he levered himself off the ground, and assumed a kneeling position to present as small a target as possible. His forearm across one knee to steady his aim, he pointed the gun at the Apache on his left who was only twenty yards away, his lips and teeth contorted into a lupine snarl. Simultaneously, he was aware of the other Apache, a little further off but closing fast.

He fired at the same moment his chosen target released an arrow and, as, though transfixed, watched the missile speeding towards him. He didn't move quickly enough and the point bit into his shoulder. Ignoring the pain, he snapped off the shaft quickly and forced himself to concentrate. Though blood was pouring from his arm where Gannon's bullet had entered, the Indian was still coming. Once again, Gannon raised the Peacemaker and fired. This time his bullet burrowed into the Apache's forehead and pierced his brain. He dropped right in his tracks.

While the buck was falling, Gannon hauled himself to his feet and faced the second Apache. Before he could focus properly, he felt a sharp pain in his side as another arrow grazed him. Enraged by pain, he knew he had to direct that rage or he'd be a goner. His eyes blazed defiance at the Apache who was only a few feet away. There was a moment of recognition as he raised the gun. But, constricted by the speed of the onslaught, he managed only a desultory aim before he pulled the trigger.

Chato still came on. Like two stags, head on in a fight, their bodies clashed together. Arms and legs entangled as they went down struggling for dominance. Gannon, conscious he was badly wounded and lacking the strength to put up much of a fight, figured it was the end for him, and any resistance only token.

Chato's knife rose out of the mêlée, the blade sparkling in a dancing celebration of light and life, not the dark promise it intended to deliver. Determined he wasn't going without a fight, Gannon reached up and grasped the Apache's wrist. He managed to prevent the weapon plunging, and couldn't figure why the downward force in the Apache's arm was rapidly diminishing so that he was able to maintain a tenuous equilibrium.

Then, just as he thought he was holding his own, a red mist spread over his right eye clouding his vision. He figured it was a sign he must be dying, his body processes shutting down. The arrow must have touched a vital organ after all. His main thought, in what he imagined must be his final moments, was for Billy; at least he'd given his son the chance of life.

Yet, one eye seemed to be functioning perfectly well. He glimpsed a red patch on Chato's shirt near the shoulder. His bullet must have wounded him there. Dark red blood was flowing from the wound. Hope resurged with the realization the the red mist obscuring his right eye must be blood from the wound falling down on to his face. Like himself, Chato was badly wounded, and probably weakening as quickly. Perhaps there was a chance he could overcome the Apache after all. That thought gave him the strength to force the knife sideways, thrust Chato's body off his own and roll away.

On all fours, he scrambled for his gun, found it, grasped it in one hand and pushed himself on to his knees. Still kneeling, he twisted, pointed the Peacemaker at Chato and prepared to finish it. Meanwhile the chief had fallen on his belly and was trying to crawl towards him. The knife was in his hand, but only his eyes retained the will to use it; his body, weakened by his wound, lacked the wherewithal.

Gannon's trigger finger was flexing when, at the edge of his vision, his eye caught a movement and his heart sank. Was another Apache left out there and preparing to attack him? Had all this effort been for nothing? Fearing his moment of triumph was about to be snatched away, he swung his gun towards the movement.

An Apache boy was standing twenty yards off. He was a motionless spectator, holding the reins of two mustangs as he drank in the tableau before him with a miserable expression. Detecting not the slightest sign of aggression, nor any sign he was armed, Gannon's attention flickered between the chief and the new arrival, not knowing where to settle.

'No,' Chato yelled, louder than Gannon thought he could have managed. He threw the knife away in a gesture of complete surrender.

Gannon saw the hate in the chief's eyes die away. It was replaced by a look of fear but he didn't have time to dwell on the reasons. He was realizing it was the same boy he'd seen next to Chato in the camp. He must have been around Billy's age, certainly not yet mature enough to become a fully-fledged Apache warrior. He'd probably been left to look after their horses while they attacked the whiteman but he had grown curious and disobeyed orders.

'Kill me, Gannon, not my son. He is not yet a warrior.'

Chato's changed demeanour made sense now. There was no pride left in his voice. To plead with your enemy in such a way was a weakness in Apache eyes, unbecoming even in a squaw. Gannon realized the effort it must have taken for the Apache chief to beg, especially in front of his son. It made him seem more human, a creature of emotion, not just the desert scavenger of repute.

Gannon swung the gun back and pointed it at the chief's head, forcing himself to remember this was the guerrilla fighter who terrorized the south-west, whose kind had tortured the little girl he'd had to kill. He didn't look so much now. One shot would finish him and there were men who would relish the chance; they wouldn't hesitate for a moment to blow Chato's head off.

He tried to pull the trigger but his eyes, as though to a magnet, were compelled towards the boy, who was rooted to the spot, in fear for his father's life. He wondered if it was the fact Chato was helpless, or that the boy reminded him he had a son of his own, which was making him hesitate. He knew the priest, who had sacrificed his life for his own son, would surely have argued for mercy.

He would probably never understand exactly why, but he couldn't do it and live with it afterwards. His conscience was already overburdened. Slowly, he eased off on the trigger and let his arm drop to his side, the Peacemaker hanging limply from his hand like a useless appendage.

He motioned to the Apache boy who ran to his father's side, and bent over him solicitously. He was conscious of his own injuries – the pain from the broken arrow protruding from his shoulder, the sharp nip from his side where Chato's arrow had sliced his flesh. All he wanted to do was rest but he couldn't afford to yet.

The boy helped Chato to his feet. One arm round his father's waist, he guided him towards Gannon. They halted a few paces away. The chief was staring at his adversary with incredulity and relief. He appeared the antithesis of the fearsome warrior of a few minutes ago.

When, at last, he found his voice he said, 'We do not expect favours from the white eyes. But the boy is my son and I thank you for his life.'

'There's a condition,' Gannon said. 'And you won't like it.'

Chato nodded. 'For the boy's life, it will be nothing.'

'Then take what's left of your men back to the reservation. Try one more time. If you kill again after I've spared you today, it will sit too heavy with my conscience.'

'It will be as you say,' Chato said. 'One more time I will try.'

As they passed close to Gannon on the way to the horses the chief, leaning on his son for support, paused.

'Why,' he asked, 'when already you have killed half my men?'

Gannon sighed. 'Maybe there's a second chance for all of us. Besides, I know there's been faults on both sides.'

'Mostly on the white's side,' Chato said ruefully. 'But I will keep my promise to Gannon. He has shown he has honour.'

Father and son continued together towards the horses. Gannon, touched by the boy's concern for the chief, called after them.

'The day of the Apache is done, Chato. Give up the war trail and let your son have a long life.'

The boy helped his father on to a horse and climbed up behind him. With his arms protectively encircling his father's waist, they cantered back to where Gannon was standing. Behind their horse, they were trailing a mustang. The boy, obeying his father's command, reached down and gave the free reins to the whiteman. The chief's eyes met Gannon's for the final time. Then he raised his hand in farewell and man and boy rode off towards the hills which had been their home for generations before the whiteman's arrival.

Gannon, leaning on the mustang's flank, watched them go, hoping he'd made the right decision. He felt he had but only time would tell whether his mercy had been misguided. It had given Chato something to think about, that was for certain; the chief's wonderment at his restraint was testimony to that. But there was no time to dwell on those matters because pain from his wounds, masked by pure adrenalin whilst he'd been fighting, was resurfacing with a vengeance and he needed a doctor.

He had no real inclination to head back to the town to find one. Far better to ride on, avoid the memories, the feelings of what might have been, which the town held for him. Necessity though, in the form of those wounds, made a return imperative. Reluctantly, apprehensive about the embarrassment he was sure awaited him there, he climbed on the horse and began the ride back.

16

Halfway into the ride, Gannon saw the dust cloud heading out of Tucson, and guessed Billy's return must have initiated a rescue party. That was confirmed when the amorphous cloud gradually transformed into shapes of heavily-armed men coming towards him at speed. It seemed ironic to him that, like everything in his life, it was coming too late to make a difference, and that all their fuss and bother was for nothing.

He reined in and waited as they came to a halt in front of him, horses kicking up dust which got up his nose and into his throat making him cough, which didn't help his pain any. One look at their faces told him they were psyching themselves up for a fight, ready to strike back at the Apaches who periodically terrorized their territory and undermined their sense of security.

'Where are those Injuns?' one of them snapped, his impatience giving no cognizance to Gannon's wounds.

'How come you're still alive?' another, whose lower lip curled stupidly downwards, followed up before he could answer the first question.

'Sorry to disappoint you,' Gannon answered, jerking a thumb. 'But you'll find five dead 'paches back there who tried to make sure I wasn't alive.' He paused, let that sink in, then added, 'It's all over fellers. You can head back home.'

Some of them looked relieved, others disappointed there wasn't going to be a chance for the retribution they felt was their right, or the opportunity to make a name for themselves in the territory as the men who'd mopped up Chato's bunch. Those were the kind that looked at him as though he was talking nonsense, indulging in self-aggrandizement. The doubting silence was embarrassing until someone broke it.

'Billy says you blew the varmints up in their nest. Chato one of them, was he?'

'Billy's right,' he answered irritably, not pleased at their indifference to his wounds and debility. 'And no, Chato wasn't one of them. I let him and his son ride away on the promise he'll go back to the reservation with what's left of his men.'

There was a low murmur of disbelief. Gannon could almost understand their scepticism, especially when it came to his acceptance of the word of an Apache who'd broken promises in the past. Some of the party would think he was downright lying about the whole thing but just weren't saying it outright.

'He'll go back, you'll see!' he reiterated firmly, wincing at the sudden jab of pain from his shoulder.

'The man's bad wounded,' a sensible voice opined. 'Gotta get him back to town before he bleeds to death. A few of us will go take a look at those dead bucks. The rest can go back with this feller.'

That seemed to suit the majority and Gannon too, who was peeved at being interrogated by those would-be heroes when he just wanted to get back to town to have his wounds tended and get some rest. Without any more delay they split up, half the men escorting him to Tucson.

As he rode with them, he decided perhaps it was only natural they should doubt that one man would blow up half those Chiricahuas then triumph against five mounted Apaches bent on revenge. Fortunately, the dead bodies would confirm his story for the doubters and give more credence to his statement that Chato would return to the reservation.

Entering the town's main drag, he was just about done in, but he did notice Billy and his stepfather on the steps of the store watching the incoming riders. When he saw Gannon amongst the party, the boy didn't hesitate. Running staight into the street, he followed the men, doing his best to keep pace, and finally catching up as they reached the doctor's surgery. As two men helped Gannon off the mustang the boy watched anxiously, eyes widening when he saw the broken arrow shaft in his shoulder, the blood-soaked shirt.

'Are you badly wounded?' he asked when Gannon raised his head to look at him. 'You ain't going to die, are you?'

Gannon just smiled down at him as one of his helpers propped him against the wall while the other rapped on the doctor's door.

'Just a little weak, son,' he stated, touched by his

concern and the incipient tears glistening at the corners of his eyes which he was doing his best to keep in check.

Billy's worried expression eased a little. 'Did you kill 'em all?' he asked, awe in his voice. 'I thought there were too many. I thought they would kill you.'

Just for a moment Gannon thought he heard something of himself in the boy, saw something in his eyes, the lure of the wild perhaps.

'I ain't proud of it,' he muttered. 'It ain't a thing to be proud of. It had to be done, was all. Remember that.'

'He will!'

The booming voice belonged to Frank Trueman who had followed Billy and was leaning on his crutch a little way along the sidewalk. Gannon recalled their last meeting, the rough treatment he had meted out, and figured the man had a genuine gripe against him.

'I'm sorry for . . . I thought—'

'No need for that!' Trueman cut him off as Billy, wondering what it was all about, looked from one adult to the other. 'My pride hurt more than the bruise. Whatever, the boy told me what you did and that makes everything right with me. Want to thank you, Jim.'

Gannon managed to return his grin. He figured Trueman was a feller who lived up to his name. Billy was lucky to have been under his influence in his formative years. He wondered if he could have done as good a job with the boy. He figured maybe now, but not before.

Their reacquainting ended as the doctor, a small, fussy individual, opened the door. He took one look at

Gannon and urged the fellow who'd been knocking to bring the wounded man inside. Billy watched him being helped over the threshold.

'Thanks for getting me away, Mr Gannon,' he called after him.

He remembered those words as the doctor was extracting the shaft and arrow head because they made the pain worthwhile. When he was bandaged up, and lying in the small back room where the doc kindly said he could stay while he recuperated, they remained in his mind as a source of comfort.

Yet, before he drifted off to sleep his regrets returned, Billy addressing him as 'Mister' Gannon the catalyst for them. Even though Billy was ignorant of their relationship and he knew he had no right to expect more, it had seemed so cold and distant, so formal, used by a son to his father.

He slept the clock round, and felt better for it, though his wounds were sore when he tried to move. The doctor examined him and told him he'd be fit to ride within a week, but he'd have to take it real easy for a while. Luckily for him, it seemed the wounds were clean and the arrows had done no serious damage.

At noon, the doctor's wife brought him a tray with home-made soup and stew which he wolfed down. Replete, he put the empty dishes aside, lay back on the pillows and turned his mind to his future plans. A light tapping on the door, however, soon broke his concentration. Thinking it must be the doc's wife returning for the dishes, he called out for her to enter.

The door opened slowly. When he looked up, he was

surprised to see Mary slip into the room and stand hesitantly near the doorway. Shafts of sunlight from the window, slanting across the room, caught her hair, giving it an extra sheen as though her head were encircled by a halo. For a moment he wondered if she were real, or a trick of his imagination.

'Come in, Mary,' he said, recovering his wits.

She made to move forward but hesitated. 'You're not angry?'

'Angry, Mary?'

Then he remembered how he'd treated her in her own home last time they'd spoken and was ashamed.

'It was drink. And the surprise of hearing about Billy,' he muttered. 'Forgive me for that please, Mary.'

He beckoned with his hand and she came forward, then settled on the chair beside his bed. She studied his bandages silently, as though reluctant to meet his gaze. Finally, she dragged her eyes up to meet his own. They lingered only a moment before dropping again. Then she covered her face with her hands and started to sob.

Gannon didn't know what to say. All he could do was mutter. 'Mary, what is it? The boy is OK, isn't he?'

'He's fine,' she said, between her sobs. 'It's not that .... It's those things I said to you. And you saved his life ... risked your own ... didn't have to. I never told you ... about him.'

'That's not how it was at all,' he said, hanging his head. 'Truth be told, you were right about me all along. It took your words the other day to finally make me see myself clear. I did it for me Mary, to ease my conscience, to make up for ...' He hesitated, thinking about how he'd left her so casually, the son he hadn't known about or seen grow up, the wild days, the little girl he'd had to shoot, the priest he'd let down . . . .

'To make up for everything, Mary, every damn, lousy thing!'

She dried her eyes on a handkerchief. She was looking at him now and he knew, like him, she was remembering the old days.

'Funny how things work out,' she said softly as she recovered some composure.

He sighed, knowing she was referring to what they'd once been to each other before he'd blown it.

'Guess Billy was the good thing to come out of our time, and in Frank you got a better husband than I would ever have made. He did a good job bringing the boy up. I can see that.'

'Yes,' she said. 'I guess I have been lucky. But you Jim, what will you do now? Have you any plans?'

'Been lying here thinking on it.'

She looked down at her hands, seeking the right nuances for what she had to say. 'Frank and me, we'd like you to stay on. We agreed we'd tell Billy you're his father. Frank says he can get you a good job. Things will be better for you now.'

When she raised her eyes again, he was smiling but shaking his head. 'Wouldn't work,' he said. 'I'm grateful to the both of you, but it wouldn't work.'

'Why, Jim? We can make it work, can't we?'

He stared at the far corner of the ceiling, as though he was trying to see the future there. He daren't look at her straight because he didn't want her to see how touched he was by the offer. Deep down, he knew that his first reaction was the right one, and was best for all of them.

'Wouldn't be fair on Billy or your husband, not yet. The boy's head would be muddled. Frank's done all right on his own. Maybe one day I can come back and we can tell Billy I'm his father.'

As he finished speaking, their eyes met. Mary nodded affirmatively, seeing the sense in his argument, thinking what was best for Billy.

'You're leaving, then,' she said, and he knew from her voice, the way she was looking at him, she was sad.

'Yes, gonna try to make something decent of myself before it's too late. I was edging that way before I came back here. Now I got to be something the boy can be proud of when the time comes for him to know me properly.'

'Maybe what happened here was meant,' she speculated, wistfully. 'There was a purpose to it.'

'Who knows? I knew a priest who might have said so. In a roundabout way it was him sent me back here to Tucson.'

Mary rose from the chair. 'Then I'm grateful to that priest whoever he was.' She leaned over him and kissed him lightly on the forehead. 'Just remember Jim, my prayers will always be with you wherever you are.'

A tear dropped on to his brow but, before he could say anything, she was heading for the door and, as she exited, she didn't look back.

17

While he was recovering, Frank Trueman visited him at the doctor's whenever he could spare time from the store. On one occasion, just as Mary had done, he tried to persuade him to stay on but received the same answer. During his visits, he grew to like the man more and more, in spite of the fact he was occupying a role, as husband and father, which might have been his had he been a different character in the old days. In fact, he found it difficult to harbour any resentment against Frank. He knew his own past had been reckless and, when he compared it to the man's proven steadfastness, felt undeserving.

One day, when he was feeling much better in himself, the door opened and Billy was there with his stepfather. He'd fattened up and looked a lot healthier, so obviously he was none the worse for his trials. Gannon hoped, after what the boy had seen of death and torture, his soul was in equally good health, resilient enough to recover from the psychological blows no young boy should have had to bear. He figured Frank Trueman was the man to see Billy through the aftermath, and he didn't intend to give his son the additional problem of suddenly finding he was his blood father. At his delicate age it might cause other problems.

Billy rushed in ahead of Frank and stood close to the bed his eyes shining with a kind of admiration as he looked at Gannon. It was plain he was bursting to speak. Frank Trueman approached behind the boy and leaned forward on his crutch. There was a wide grin on his face too.

'Which cat got the milk?' Gannon asked. 'The big one or the little one?'

'Tell him, Billy,' Frank said, 'before you bust a gut.'

'Chato's back on the reservation,' Billy blurted out, hardly pausing for breath. 'They say you're a hero now.'

'Hope he stays there,' Gannon said, genuinely relieved.

It was good news which vindicated him in the eyes of the townsfolk, he supposed. That was pleasing, especially since his son must have heard the doubters, but he was embarrassed about the hero tag, knowing his own failures too well to consider himself one. He went quiet and Frank sensed he was uncomfortable with that, and wouldn't want Billy to press it.

'We were on our way to the store but stopped off to let you know,' he stated, adding tactfully, 'Come on Billy, Jim still needs to rest and you have your chores.'

Billy went reluctantly towards the door. Frank let him go out first, paused, then turned back to face Gannon and winked.

'Gonna be hard work being a hero,' he said, good humouredly.

'Get out of here, Frank!' Gannon snorted, 'Before I turn yeller and puke all over the doc's floor.'

Alone in the quiet of the room, Gannon had time to reflect and absorb the implications of what Frank had just told him. He was pleased Chato had kept his word and gone back to the reservation. Trouble was, it sounded as if his return was hot news and there would be a lot of fuss about it, at least for a while, and that was the last thing he wanted.

Billy's good opinion of him was all he desired, all he could ever have hoped for. He didn't want the fuss, especially when he knew that if he was a hero at all, it was the flawed variety. Worse, if he remained too long and public acclaim grew too widespread, someone might recognize him from the past, and reveal what kind of man he had been. For Billy's sake mostly, but for his own too, he didn't want that. The best thing all round would be to ride on now, today. Without his presence to fuel it, the episode would die a quicker death.

When the doctor learned of his decision, he said he'd be fit to ride but not to overdo it. Gannon thanked him for his ministrations, offering him money, which he refused, saying he'd already paid him by getting those Apaches back on the reservation.

Once he was ready, he made his way to the stables as quickly as he could. Unfortunately the sling on his arm drew eyes and he had to endure mild back-slapping and compliments from citizens who recognized him. But he didn't stop and the stable hand took only perfunctory notice of him as he helped him saddle up. Once the animal was ready, he led it through the back doors of the stable into a deserted street.

Pleased to have made it that far without too much embarrassment, he put his foot in the stirrup and prepared to mount the mustang. Before he could complete the action, a voice spoke to his back. He froze mid-motion as though the words were a knife piercing him.

'You just going to leave, aren't you, without even saying goodbye?'

Like a thief caught in a crime, he took his foot slowly out of the stirrup and turned to face his son. Billy's lower lip was curled downwards and he was rhythmically poking his toe into the dust, not looking in Gannon's direction.

Inwardly, Gannon groaned. This was the last thing he'd wanted but he knew he'd have to deal with it. Licking the dryness from his lips, he walked towards his son and stood in front of him, his mind searching for the right words.

'You're my friend, Billy,' he said finally. 'Good friends don't have to say goodbye. Besides one day, when you're a bit older, I'll be coming back.'

Billy's head lifted. His toe ceased its poking. He was studying Gannon's face, a spark of humour coming into his own.

'You're really coming back one day?'

Gannon knelt down beside him. 'You got my word on it, but it ain't all one way. You've gotta make me a couple of promises.'

'Sure I will,' Billy said smiling. 'We're friends, ain't

we? What do you want me to promise?'

'Just take care of your ma and pa son. You see I ain't met many women as good as your ma and I never met a man like your pa. Wish I was more like him.'

'But . . . but they say you're a hero.'

Gannon's face flushed. 'There's things you don't know, Billy. In my time I've been a bad man, done bad things and now I'm trying to be a better man. Frank, your pa, he's always been a good man I reckon, and he got that leg proving how much he thinks of you.'

'I guess,' Billy said, then looked straight at him, the question transparent in his own eyes before he voiced it. 'What bad things did you do?'

Gannon smiled. 'All you gotta know is I'm trying to be better. One day, you'll understand that.'

He made to rise but Billy moved quicker, throwing his arms round his neck. When he eventually released him Gannon stood up, turned quickly away and headed back to his horse.

'Remember what I told you, Billy,' he shouted with one last look at his son before mounting up and spurring his horse.

It was only when he was miles clear of the town that he dared look back. A lot had happened to him but he felt better than he had in a long time, as though the burrs were at last out from under his saddle. Whether by accident or design, that priest had been right. It was never too late to try to right a wrong.